Ivar,
Takk
Gud

ALSO BY
VERNON J. HENDRIX

Barsabas

Ivar,
Takk
Gud

A Novel by
Vernon J. Hendrix, M.D.

Meetinghouse Books
PROVIDENCE HOUSE PUBLISHERS
FRANKLIN, TENNESSEE

Printed in the United States of America

05   04   03   02   01   1   2   3   4   5

Library of Congress Catalog Card Number: 2001087994

ISBN: 1-57736-234-9

Cover design by Gary Bozeman
Cover photo © 2001—Corbis

This story is entirely fictional. Any similarity to actual people, living or dead, is purely coincidental. It is meant neither to harm nor to injure anyone. This tale is the product of the author's imagination; it is taken from events that historically could have happened, but may not have occurred in real life. Although the names of the places exist, the events as told in the story may not have actually happened.

With the passage of time, any parallelism between events held by members of some families, living or dead, should be considered a pure coincidence. As years pass, those lives touched by points in the past grow in a geometric fashion. No attempt should be made to identify certain individuals as described in the story with people in real life.

Linkage of fiction and fact is neither intended nor implied. This story is fiction.

 Meetinghouse Books
PROVIDENCE HOUSE PUBLISHERS
238 Seaboard Lane • Franklin, Tennessee 37067
800-321-5692
www.providencehouse.com

To God

And God said,
Let us make man in our image,
after our likeness: and let them have dominion over the fish of the sea,
and over the fowl of the air, and over the cattle, and over all the earth,
and over every creeping thing that creepeth upon the earth.

—Genesis 1:26—

CHAPTER ONE

*It is a wise child that
knows his own father.*

—*The Odyssey,* Homer—

"ARE YOU MY DADDY?"

That one question is as far back in my memory as I can retrieve. It must have occurred sometime when I was about three years old. Even though I am now a full sixteen years old, this exact thought is indelibly imprinted in my mind as if it were yesterday.

Maybe the image of this event is so clear in my mind because it has shaped my whole life. Although I do not constantly dwell on this memory, I realize that I have always had questions about myself, about my origins, about my true family, and about the purpose of my creation.

To explain, let me go back to that earliest of memories, to that question which is at the first pinpoint of my mind.

The gentle and benevolent appearing gray-haired man bent over the three-year-old boy on the dock between the storage shed and the moored coastal steamer. The youngster was me. I do not remember how I came to be at the wharf that day, who accompanied me, or why I was there. Nearly everything that came to Kirkenes, Norway, my home, came by way of small freighters. This vessel's arrival was the high point of the day. The ship was the very lifeblood connection between the remote village of Kirkenes and the rest of the world.

Hence, I guess that as a small child I felt as if that one void in my life, "my Daddy," would be brought to me by the steamer.

It seemed natural that I would ask the stranger who had just walked down the ship's gangway, "Are you my Daddy?"

The elderly man bent low over me. Startled by this direct question from me, he slowly answered, "No, I am not your father, but I wish that I were because you seem to be very smart. I would be so proud if you were my son. You are everything that one could ask for in a boy."

I could not understand the English spoken very well by the gentleman. However, I could sense that his answer was a negative. I could perceive a touch of sadness on his part, seeing a single tear course down his cheek before his finger cleared it away. Evidently, we felt a uniform pain in the moment. One boy was searching for a void in his young life, and the stranger, feeling the lad's meaningful and significant quest, was touched by the enormity of what could be behind the boy's question.

The elderly American savored the moment. To think that at the northern terminal of the Norwegian coastal voyage system, here in a remote arctic port, somewhere above the tree line, a primeval question had been put to him by a small boy. The boy, me, was searching for his father. Yet, now that I am sixteen years old, I can understand the stranger's full emotion. The American understood my question, even in the Norwegian language. He sensed the generic question beyond the obvious. He fully realized that the interrogation was from the depths of the soul of mankind at the time of creation. I know now that the American felt more than I did about the probing comment I threw at him about our relationship. The American was sensitive enough to read the symbolism into this first comment addressed to him upon stepping foot on Kirkenes soil.

"Are you my Daddy?"

The adult saw beneath the surface. He virtually tasted the inner core of mankind asking the same question down through the annals of history.

To me, at the time, a father meant love, security, family, guidance, and companionship. My only source of these intangibles was my mother. Although she cherished me to the fullest, she could not round out the role of a father. Even at age three, I knew that something was missing.

At the time of asking the American whether or not he was my father, I had not posed the question to my mother. Later on, when I directly asked her about my father and who I was, my mother would always answer by saying, "You are Ivar, Takk Gud." Over time I had heard the phrase, "You are Ivar, Takk Gud" so many times that I came to feel that my name was truly "Ivar, Takk Gud."

Years later, probably when I was about eight, I understood that my real name was Ivar Enge. I knew that what my mother had originally said was that I was "Ivar, Thank God." She had originally offered her own image of me as a son, a child given to her by an ever loving God, a boy filling her lonesome life with joy and with laughter. She never volunteered information about my true father. Either the situation was too painful or she was ashamed of her downfall. My last name was Enge. That was the same last name of my mother, Ingrid Enge. Hence, there was no linkage with a father figure. At no time when I was growing up did the village conversation bring up any reference to my father. Either they did not know or they were all part of the big mystery.

In my mind, I was Ivar, Takk Gud or Ivar Enge.

It did not change my existence. I was a healthy Norwegian boy, I had a loving mother, I always had plenty to eat, and my clothes kept me reasonably warm. My mother and I shared a small three-room house downhill from the Kirkenes square. In the immediate area were plenty of playmates. Although I was poor, I was rich. To a child, the assessment of happiness does not depend on the Norwegian krona. The coin of the realm is strictly an avenue to get necessities. Even though I am now sixteen, I can see what is important. My needs are Spartan.

In saying to me, "You are Ivar, Takk Gud," my mother was inadvertently teaching me more than maybe she realized. To give thanks to God, in understanding that my very being came as a gift from the Almighty, was a wonderful way of a mother giving a son something more than knowledge of a father I never knew. She must have had her reasons for never discussing my biological father. I must respect her decision. Instead, I came to realize that I am part of the Lord's creation. He is my Father. He has given me total dominion over creation. In more ways than one, I am Ivar, Takk Gud. My given name of Ivar is no greater nor lesser than the name, Thank God. Even though my early misunderstanding of my name at first confused me, I am now grateful of the error because I now know that I am God's child. And for that, I thank God.

I never saw the American gentleman again. I trust that the fleeting episode of our meeting on the dock where the ship moored carried some special significance to him. I distinctly remembered the tear rolling down his cheek. I understand that he may have interpreted the moment entirely different than I did. Yet, it was so meaningful to me that it is my first memory in life. In that instance, I was seeking a father I already had. In the lapse of thirteen years, I wonder if he remembers our exchange, and I hope that our dialogue was a seedling sprouting into a tree of memory to him.

Most people, when they tell the story of their youth, describe their hometown as just any other village on the map. Although I did not know it at the time, Kirkenes is far from being a carbon copy of similar towns. For one thing, Kirkenes is near the seventy degrees north latitude. Not only is Kirkenes far above the Arctic Circle, the small village is the last point of habitation on the Arctic Ocean before crossing over the border into Russian territory. From the hill near my house, I can see the two miles to the old border checkpoint. The coast of Norway extends so far to the east that my home in Kirkenes is farther east than Istanbul, Turkey. The population of the area is never over five thousand people, even in the summer. This small size permitted me to know everybody, to explore every nook and cranny, and to be reasonably safe as long as I stayed away from the water.

By the time I was four years old, I knew the row of small houses where I lived. The neighbors threw their windows open during the long summer days. The sun never set for seventy days of the summer. People enjoyed the outdoors. Dogs roamed the yards and occasionally jumped the small wooden fences. Roosters crowed at all hours of the day, confused by their biological clocks. Instinctively, I knew which neighbors would welcome me on the rare times when I thought I had escaped my mother's eye. Yards were small, and the residences were tiny; the need to conserve heat during the winter dictated their miniature proportions.

The roads were all gravel. Because of the shifting of the surface in the extremes of winter, no pavement of any kind could be employed. This left a supply of mud for a young boy to revel in when not watched. I remember several well-worn holes that held a particular attraction for me. At age four, keeping mud off of my clothes was not important to me. In the yards there were no trees. Several neighbors always planted a small shrub for the summer in the few spots where they had added topsoil over the bedrock granite tundra. They understood that the small bushes would be doomed by the onset of the early winter; nevertheless, they emotionally needed to see something growing. Moss gave the rocks some color. In late May, a sparse crop of wild flowers dotted the little areas where dirt had accumulated. By age four the only tree I remember was of the imported variety, brought in by the ships at Christmas time.

When I think back about the village, I can understand why all the buildings were erected so close together. From my three-room house to the Rica Hotel, where my mother worked, the distance was less than two hundred meters. The extreme cold of the long winters ruled life. From November 23 until March 8 each year, darkness pervaded the land. Mix the dark with minus ten degrees centigrade temperatures, along with winds off the Varanger Fjord at thirty miles per hour, and any walk made outdoors was only made when deemed vitally necessary. Now that I am sixteen years old, I can see these things clearly. Yet, in the eyes of a preschool child, Kirkenes was my world.

My mother, a tall statuesque Nordic woman, worked at the sixteen room Rica Hotel. Her duties at the Rica consisted of everything from cleaning the rooms to serving behind the front desk. During mealtime she acted as a waitress in the small dining room. From nine o'clock in the morning until five o'clock in the afternoon, my mother worked at any job that needed to be done. It was not unusual for my mother to bring home kitchen leftovers from the Rica Hotel at the end of the work day. I do not know the arrangement for the food, other than it came to be accepted. On many days she would take our dirty clothes with her when she went to work. Our clothes were washed and dried along with the hotel linens at the hotel site. Even while very young, I remember standing outside the vents of the laundry room, relishing the warm air blown out as vented vapor into the arctic air.

Most of the time when my mother picked me up from the day care center, we went the short three blocks to our home. The three room, gingerbread cottage consisted of a small kitchen adjoining a living area. In the living area, two pull-down convertible beds became our bedroom. Off of this area was a small bathroom, making the full square of the one-story wooden house. Our only storage area was above the high pitched roof, accessible by a pull-down telescoping wooden staircase. Outside the double-pane glass storm windows, my mother hung window level pots during the summer containing hardy blooming plants whose flowers gave a joyous touch of color. Our only source of heat were floor-level electric space heaters. The house was not big enough for a fireplace. Wood was too scarce, anyway, and had to be imported by ship. Rarely did the electricity fail. If that happened, we both slept in the small lobby of the Rica Hotel. The diminutive cubic volume of our house meant that any trapped heat quickly made the house reasonably cozy by Norwegian standards.

As you can quickly judge, from the time I was three until six years old, my mother and I were not rich by any means. Nevertheless, we had all the basics. Now that I am sixteen years old and I look back on my mother's life, I can see how meager we lived. She considered everyone in the entire village to be her friends. Her social outlet was the sole Lutheran church sitting high on the granite knoll, one block from the Kirkenes square and overlooking the long and wide fjord coursing to the north, out into the expansive Arctic Ocean.

At no time can I remember her entertaining a male friend. With her good features and happy disposition, however I feel certain that she had possibilities. If this were the case, she delegated all contacts to the workplace and to daylight hours. As I look back in time, I cannot remember her sitting with any one particular person in church. Unlike many, we had no usual designated pew. In good weather we did not walk to the church with any certain group. Instead we ambled along with anybody going that way.

Sunday was centered around church. Saturdays, however, were the times most of my fun memories were built around. Totally dependent on weather, my mother and I spent picnic journeys to the surrounding spots of interest. The massive ship drydock yards, the airfield, the old train railbed leading to the abandoned open-pit nickel mines, the cargo wharf of the freighters, and the checkpoint of the Russian border on the Pasvikelven River were all within walking distance. Sometimes others would go with us. To me, it made little difference. It took all day to walk to the site, to listen as my mother told me stories about the area, to let a child's imagination fantasize the tale into a wonderful adventure, to eat a prepared lunch in the fields or perched upon a rock. At the end of the day, as I fell asleep exhausted, magnificent stories magically continued in my dreams. . . . I was poor, but I was rich.

Winter turned the pages of life. A whole new scheme had to be adopted when the cold and darkness came. All attention turned to books. Only by reading, at first my mother reading to me, and later, my rooting out the tales by myself, could the quest for boyhood adventure be satisfied. Darkness brought out the self-reliance of the proud Norwegian. Even by age six, I felt comfortable on both skis and snowshoes. Indoors we devised games, relished conversation, retold the ancient sagas of the Norse era, and formulated our tempered self-images as survivors.

The image of the old man's tear rolling down his cheek often returned to my mind during the darkness of the Norwegian winters. I do not know exactly what he was thinking at the time. Was the tear shed out of pity, when he really did not know of my plight, a distressed situation he could not have envisioned? All I understood at the time was the fact that the ship brought everything needed to Kirkenes. I needed a father. If this man got off the ship, then I wanted to inquire if he were possibly my father. To a three-year-old boy, this is sound reasoning. Was the man's tear for all the generic children of the world facing this dilemma? Was there an unknown thorn in the elderly person's life that triggered a long past painful recall? I will never know. Yet, he has left me with my precious memory. Although wiped from his face, that tear lives on and on in my sixteen-year-old brain.

I would never have the nerve to confront my mother. She bore me. She gave me life. She nursed me. Our existence together was happy as only in childhood one can measure joy. We do not have adult yardsticks to grade happiness. As children our contentment is pure. We are allowed to savor delightful life without the blurring shade of grays and off-whites that cloud the minds of adults.

My mother did not abort me from the womb. Instead, she chose to teach a son the meaning of sacrificial love. And, now at age sixteen, I recognize her sacrifice. She has given me the name of Ivar, Takk Gud. I feel that, between my mother and God, I have been given that most precious gift of life. Part of me is Takk Gud. . . .

CHAPTER TWO

Youth comes but once in a lifetime.
—*Hyperion,* Longfellow—

ON THE HIGHEST HILL IN KIRKENES, ON THE ROUTE BETWEEN the Rica Hotel and my modest home, stands a larger-than-life monument to the Soviet soldiers who liberated my area from the occupying Nazi military in the 1940s. Starting with several large square granite steps as a base, followed by a pedestal column, and ending with a towering depiction of an armed Russian soldier in uniform facing to the southwest, the site is an enduring evidence of the gratitude of the Norwegian people.

First introduced to this interesting site by my mother, it became one of our favorite places to take a small basket of food from our kitchen on those summer evenings. To eat outdoors and to have the appetite of a boy between the ages of six and nine adds to the memory of the monument. During those years, every minute spent at the site was spent in confusion between what was more important—playing or eating. I must now confess that as a child in that age range the true meaning behind the statue did not register in my thoughts. The scars and the pain of previous generations are not inflicted necessarily upon the games of the young. The inert and immobile face of the Soviet soldier neither had my hunger nor smiled at my delight in childhood games. I now realize these jaunts for my mother satisfied a degree of relief from the boredom of a repetitive ritual. In the fresh air coming off the Varanger Fjord, possibly she was seeking to clear the cobwebs from her brain of a life closing down on her with each tick of the clock. Now that

I am sixteen, I can imagine the sullen thoughts she must have shared with the gloomy statue. I wish that I possessed the power to turn back the hands of time and to erase those troubles from my mother's shoulders. Meanwhile, the morose Russian monument stared at his German foe, as Don Quixote gazed at the windmill, an enemy now vanquished by the winds of time.

At the age of seven, I did not know. Now, I understand the huge obelisk.

In June of 1941, the German Army commanded by the Austrian General Dietl, advanced from Kirkenes on to Russian territory in the direction of Murmansk. Only going eastward a few miles from the Norwegian border, the Nazi army was stopped by Russian forces. At that point the front remained static until October 25, 1944, more than three long years. On October 25, 1944, the Russian offensive drove the German forces out of Kirkenes. Rather than provoke a retreating foe over land ravaged by a scorched earth policy, the Soviets broke off contact and permitted the Germans to leave Finmark, the northernmost province of Norway. Hence, Kirkenes was freed. The Russians passed all civil authority over to the Norwegians. Imagine the gratitude of the people of Kirkenes.

Sometime around age nine, the story of the war, the meaning of the statue, and the glory of the military became part of my childhood brain. With that came the inevitable war games of my youth. One day I would play the role of the Russian soldier; the next day I would be the dreaded German; then, my playmates would elect me to the part held in highest esteem, the Norwegian.

Recently in my thoughts, I returned my mind back to those idyllic days of summer. I wondered if my mother's almost mystical attachment to the hilltop statue could have anything to do with one of the monument's characters being my true father. I could never bring myself to ask her the direct question. Then I did the mental mathematics. Because of the dates, neither I nor my mother had even been borne at the 1944 liberation. Kirkenes was freed. I was not freed from my quest for a father. Could I be in a growth stage spurred forward by this ever plaguing question? Could the Lord be strengthening me for a coming harder test of resolve? Could my character take on the surrounding terrain and the vicissitudes of the Nordic climate, tempered for Viking sagas that faced me in later life? I pondered.

One Christmas, my eighth, my mother gave me a pair of binoculars. This was no toy. The glasses were not new. They were authentic German artillery issue with the inscription still visible. This made them so much more valuable in my eyes. How she obtained this priceless of all objects, I will never know. The surprise was almost, even as child, overwhelming. And then, disappointment hit me broadside. The arctic winter had kissed the sun goodbye on November 24. It would be totally dark until the return of the sun on March 4. The enjoyment of the binocular fascination would have to wait until light returned.

One day I was down at the freighter dock, proudly carrying my useless Christmas gift, when a ship's officer noticed my prize. Understanding that this boy cherished his toy but had yet to be enthralled by its power due to darkness, he asked the boy to wait a few minutes at the ship's gangway. Soon, the uniformed sailor returned bearing a sizeable atlas.

In his proud Norse voice, he said to me, "If you are going to be a Viking, sailing the seven seas, using the advantage powerful binoculars give you, then until daylight comes again, you will need to study these pictures. You will need to memorize all these foreign flags that fly from the stern of seagoing vessels. You will need to read other books about the various countries that run these ships. Utilize these color picture charts that allow you to recognize from the smokestack the colors and the pictures painted for all to see. With your binoculars, you will be able to see long in advance of anyone else the oncoming vessel, know its name, and have the country's identity. By studying this book, you will have the knowledge required of a sea captain from Norway."

I have often wondered if that mariner realized that his one incident stimulated an eight-year-old boy on a lifetime of ardent study, an appreciation of the power of the learning process, and the value of books. By the time daylight returned to Norway, I had the charts firmly memorized. I had gazed at the telltale smokestacks of all the vessels. As my reading skills improved, I had even learned to pronounce the names of the foreign countries.

The officer of the *Hurtigruten,* the Norwegian coastal shipping system, had given me more than a book. He had given me a practical demonstration of the power of the learning process. When daylight returned to Norway, I was ready. Armed with my precious binoculars, armed with the indexing skills to identify ships, and sensing the power that education can give, I had a new hobby.

The underground granite pits around the old Nazi cannon bunkers provided us with wonderful playgrounds. Some of the rooms for gun mounts and for storage of ammunition were larger than the living space of my house. The side walls of hard stone were rough. Because of wear, access to the inside gave ample footing. With the extreme arctic dryness, there was no green slime as one would expect in more temperate climates. These bunkers were not formed by the recession of glaciers at the end of the Ice Age. If that were the case, the cavities would be more in the form of a shallow bowl. These rooms were man-made. Nevertheless, the openings were sufficient to move explosive carts during the war years. In our play, the entrances allowed adequate light, making us one of the strongest game sites imaginable.

The children of Kirkenes were like bear cubs, protected in an underground warren from the elements, sheltered from the constant arctic winds coming off the fjord, and housed in a fairly central spot known by all the parents. Like children worldwide, "home base" was a component of our games. In our situation our shelter was an aftermath of German oppression, an offensive force employed against Norwegian people, now converted by the minds of playful youngsters into a refuge.

Out of a bloody war came a childrens' playground. At age sixteen that was a hard concept for me to totally understand. I thought life was more black and white. The realization of life as a continuum, happiness mixed with sadness, mirth blended with tears, lows counterbalanced with highs, was new to me. Only lately have I gained that maturity.

As good as the caves sound, believe me, there were many downsides. The town constable made it part of his morning rounds to check the dungeons for wandering drunks who had fallen asleep in the shelter of the rockpits. Smells of garbage, particularly old fish, had to be cleaned with industrial strength chemicals. Because of solid rock, drainage was poor. With compressed air hammers, points of water elimination had to be drilled into the hollows. In these efforts, the townspeople of Kirkenes assumed their responsibility.

However, to me at age eight, I had the perfect haven.

Rarely did I have the bunkers to myself. Nevertheless, I remember distinctly being sprawled out on the floor of the cave, gazing out the overhead opening into a late summer afternoon sky. Like eight-year-olds the world over, I was trying to form in my mind the shape of the clouds into a definitive object. This went on for as long as one's attention span can at age eight. Then my mind shifted into what made the clouds, into what changed the weather, and finally, into why did God cause such strange cloud formations. Now that I am sixteen, as I think back in time, that must have been my first spontaneous conceptual experience with attempting to understand God.

I knew that there was far more to God and to the concept of God than I was capable of knowing. Still, I remember being challenged by the Creator of the clouds, by the immensity of the sky, by the ever-changing kaleidoscope that I was watching while I was flat on my back in that solid granite bunker.

In my child's mind, I was thanking God. Today, I still thank God. And, I thank God for all the memories that have centered around my mighty granite fortress since then.

Until age nine, children were never permitted to roam very far from the settlement in the warm weather months. Understand, the word—warm—is relative. Of course, during the winter we were accompanied anywhere, the journeys being limited in both time and in distance. During the spring, summer, and autumn, when adults took us on trips into the hinterland tundra, I remember that the chaperons always carried a fully loaded, safety on, hunting rifle. Now that I think back on this custom, these weapons were of sizeable caliber. We were always told that the rifles were present because of the dangers of bears and of wolves. Never in my memory, however, did I hear of anyone being attacked by either species. At that age the only bears or wolves I had seen were of the stuffed variety on display in the shopwindows on the Kirkenes square. Maybe, the adults wanted to impress us with potential peril. I do not know. Regardless, it worked.

The greatest and very real danger to us was around water. Kirkenes arose at the very headwater of the Varanger Fjord. Adventure centered around the freighter docks, the drydock, and ship repair facilities.

Fishing vessels were constantly present. We were around people who made their living on the sea. Adult conversation focused on fish, on the catch, and on the habits of the fish harvest. Jobs in the fish factories gave employment to many of the women. Yet, the temperature of the water meant a rapid death if a child fell into the sea. Consequently, we were never allowed near those areas until we were at least twelve.

Hence, all the children of Kirkenes did not learn to swim until they were on visits to the south.

One of the jokes was, "Where are you going?"

The reply, "To the south."

Obviously, any person or object leaving Kirkenes has to go south, except for the short jaunt up the fjord into the open Arctic Ocean. Everything is to the south. Except for Svalbard or for Spitzbergen, there is no other direction.

By far, the greatest number of animals were the birds. Gannets, puffins, kittiwakes, terns, and guillemots soared on the updrafts of the winds. They nestled on the rocky cliffs, protected from all predators, except the sea eagle. Cormorant and eider duck were too numerous to count. When ledges were accessible under their nests, huge supplies of guano remained if not washed away by tidal flush. The local people had little use of the fertilizer because it is too high in nitrogen unless titrated down by sand, and then the local people have little soil in which to grow plants. Considering the difficulty and peril to harvest the guano, it is generally ignored.

The bird feathers are so bountiful. As children, we ignored them. Their only use was to adorn hats.

In Kirkenes we valued the meat of the reindeer and of the whale. Because the diet of the reindeer is primarily moss and lichen, the meat has no wild grass taste. The whale, being a mammal, has no fishy taste. The whale flesh is red meat. It has more the appearance of a round of beef. Without the interspersed fat layering of beef, the whale is pure protein and can be cooked accordingly. Certain species of whale are no longer threatened by hunting. Since Norway abides by the international restrictions on harvesting whales, the larger whales are left alone. The minke whale, however, one of the smaller species, is numerous enough to withstand limited hunts. We honor the moral stand. Seal meat and seal furs are completely restricted.

It was in this environment of innocence that I spent my youth.

CHAPTER THREE

*Sin creeps on the scene in silence
in many languages.*

—Ancient Proverb—

BEFORE BEDTIME IN THE WANING LIGHT I WAS SCANNING THE fjord with my binoculars. From my house I could not see the entire expanse of sea. Several of the neighbors' houses blocked the view. The better view was from up near the Soviet soldier's monument. Why I turned totally around to look at the statue through my binoculars, I do not know. But, I did.

At that moment outlined against the darkening sky was the figure of the uniformed town policeman. Without the uniform, I could not have told the identity of the person. He was carrying the limp body of a woman. Even with my spy glasses, I could only make out the figure being a woman by the long hair and by the outline of her dress. I watched as the constable went around the monument and into the hollow of one of the bunkers. I thought at the time that this was a strange sight to see, but I was only curious. Soon sleep overcame my thought process.

The next morning I did not think of the previous night's episode. My mother and I went through our normal routine. After a quick breakfast, she accompanied me to my primary school one block behind the Rica Hotel. I did not remember to mention anything about what I had seen the night before to my mother. My activities in the school began as was the usual.

Within an hour, however, the headmaster of the school appeared outside my class door. She summoned my teacher out into the corridor.

From my desk I could see the discussion, the horrible look on both their faces, the animated talk, and their looks of outright despair.

When my teacher returned to the class, she said, "Students. I want you to stop what you are doing. I want you to immediately go home. Do not stop along the way. Do not talk with anybody, other than your parents. Your mothers and fathers will explain why school is being closed."

I had no place to go, other than across the street to the Rica Hotel where my mother was working. When I walked in the back door leading into the lobby, I could see the mass of townspeople, many in tears. My mother was among them. She was crying. Seeing me, she turned, put her arms around my shoulders, and led me off to the side near the leather sofa.

"Mrs. Knutson is dead," she softly related to me. "Stay right here in the lobby. I will explain what happened, and we will go home as soon as I can."

I could not understand. I had never experienced anyone I knew dying. Of course, I had heard of sailors dying at sea. I knew that soldiers died in the war. But nobody I knew personally had ever died. Mrs. Knutson lived in the small house right next door. She had always shared cookies with me, knowing that I had smelled them baking in her kitchen. Although Lekamoya, Mrs. Knutson's daughter, was three years older, I had played with her since before I could remember. My name for the girl was Leki. Mrs. Knutson had always been good to me. I could not believe she was dead. In my mind, I could still see her plainly. She had always been there for me if my mother was not around. I was confused. What happens now? My mind snapped back to the scene.

The lady headmaster at school brought a red-eyed Leki into the hotel lobby and led Leki over to my mother. My mother bent down to Leki, embraced her gently, and they both cried. Instinctively, I went directly to my playmate. The three of us wept together.

Addressing the collected people, my mother said, "Leki will be staying from now on with me. I think it is best if we go home. We have some crying to do. I know that you will understand."

With that gesture, my mother gathered up her purse and herded us out the double front door of the hotel. Walking home my mother held me by the hand. With her other arm, she held Leki around the shoulder as close as she could. Little was said. We cried muffled sounds; the finality of death was not fully registered in our young minds.

As we approached our front door my mother stated, "We are home. We have each other. The two of us are now three. Leki, you will live with us. I can not replace your mother. No one can do that. But, we will lean on one another. With God's help, we will survive. Somehow we will get through these times. None of us can understand what nor why this has happened. But, with the prayers of many, we will continue on living. Leki, your mother was a fine woman. She was my best friend. Ivar and I will be here for you. Things will never be the same. But, remember you are loved."

For as long as I live, I will never forget what my mother had just said.

She said what was in her character. To a neighbor's orphaned child, she had opened her heart. In a house barely large enough to house the two of us, she had brought in Leki. With a job that barely furnished us food, she mentally had put another plate at the table. Unhesitatingly, before there was any discussion in the town, she had brought Leki home. My mother had known from previous discussions with Mrs. Knutson that she had no relatives. Evidently, the two women had consoled one another. Neither had husbands. I do not know what happened to Mr. Knutson. At no time in my memory had there been a father for Leki next door. Maybe that is why my mother and Mrs. Knutson were so close.

At one time when I was daydreaming about the community, about Mrs. Knutson and my mother, and about how the remoteness of Kirkenes brought about a closeness of the people, I had fantasized that maybe the same man had been the father of both Leki and of me. The more I thought about this idea, the more I realized that my mother and Mrs. Knutson would have never tolerated this fact. They were too close. Two women, even my mother, would never have been able to live side by side, maintain their happy relationship, and see each other on a daily basis. Quickly, I knew that this random idea was purely a result of my feelings for Leki. We had shared lunches. We had wrestled together in our games. We had enjoyed hours of games around the statue of the Soviet soldier. Leki was the older sister I never had.

Now she had come to live with us on a permanent basis.

Proudly, I pulled down the telescoping staircase into our upstairs storage area. By rearranging the stored boxes in the area, I made room for a bed. Although there was no window to the outside, it made no difference because there was no light anyway. By leaving the collapsible staircase down during the night, I had access to the toilet. Up the stairs went most of the heat. As it turned out, with my bed being upstairs, I was the one most comfortable. All in all, it gave me a sense of pride that I could signal a welcome to Leki in this way.

Through the dreary darkness of the long winter, Leki fought a battle no young girl should have to endure. Certainly, my mother made her part of our family. My mother hugged Leki as they talked over her schoolwork. My mother strove to be both mother and an older sister. Leki's moods would be as long as the black sky. Leki would go with me to school. Because she was three years older, she and I could go home together and not have to wait for my mother to get off work. Nevertheless, Leki was unpredictable. In her despondency, one day before my mother came home from work, Leki took the scissors and cut her hair off very short. On other occasions Leki would take a dislike to a dress, tear the dress apart, and end up crying uncontrollably. My mother, who had little income to replace torn clothing, never scolded Leki. My mother seemed to understand. When these events happened, she would merely take Leki in her arms and hold her close.

Some days Leki would retire up the staircase to my bed, pull the stairwell up behind her, and stay until dinnertime. Other times Leki would refuse to talk. Red-eyed from crying, Leki did not want to participate in any of the family activities. My mother always seemed to understand. I did not. When my mother sensed my frustration, she would always calm me by holding my two hands.

Looking me directly in the eyes, my mother would say, "Realize Leki's loss. Our love is all she has."

When this happened, my mother showed me her strength. She brought out the best in me. I wanted to be the big man. Whatever Leki needed from me, I wanted to give. My mother made me understand that the Lord had placed Leki in our care. To fail in any way this charge was a sin in the eyes of God. Instilling this attitude in me, my mother was building a man, and I knew it plainly at the time. She was implanting in me pride and at the same time giving Leki the love that she needed.

Leki had lost her mother, had the onset of menarche, had the three months of arctic darkness, and had the bitterness of tasting an unknown future.

At my age at the time, I could not understand all of this. I merely wanted to play along and not be the stumbling block.

CHAPTER FOUR

Know ye not that we shall judge angels?
how much more things that pertain
to this life?

—1 Corinthians 6:3—

AT AGE SIXTEEN, I HAVE SO MUCH TO LEARN, YET I AM BURDENED by facts that I do not exactly know how to handle. In the dark recesses of my memory, I vividly recall that moment when I saw the village policeman carry the limp body of a woman through the dim light into the hollow of one of the bunkers near the statue of the Soviet soldier. When this occurred, I do not remember how I decided what to do. Later, I learned that the woman was Mrs. Knutson. Maybe, it was my youth. Anyway, I told no one, even my mother. I can not recall whether my judgment was colored by the sight of the uniform of the Kirkenes policeman, by the worry that by voicing what I had seen may get my mother in trouble, by the swift unfolding of the immediate events of Leki coming to live with us, or by the total turmoil rapidly developing in my life. Regardless, in the mental fog of the time, I said nothing.

I tried to dismiss the event from my memory. Sometimes that outline of the limp woman's body would leave me for months at a time. Nevertheless, the image would invariably return. Little things, simple gestures, Leki's references would all summon the memory back. However, I never had resolution of how to exactly handle the event I had witnessed. I did have presence of mind to calculate that nobody would place any value on what a small child had seen. I had the good sense to know that to implicate the village constable would only make my mother's life more unbearable. I felt that the uniform carried authority. To go against a stronger power would hurt my mother, Leki, and myself. Consequently, I did nothing.

The passage of time seemed to make my sighting of the event even less believable. Mrs. Knutson was buried in the churchyard of the Kirkenes Luthern Church. Leki was living with us. She became as an older sister to me. I was enjoying my youth. When the image of the dead woman's body hit my consciousness, I was always able to shove it aside, awaiting a time when I was older and would have the maturity to know how to process the nightmare.

Over a span of years the disappearance of the Cold War caused even changes in the Norwegian arctic. The Russian trawlers showed signs of deterioration. Hulls took on visible rust. Engines were not maintained. The Russian crews, when they had shore leave in Kirkenes, had no money to spend. Items that they purchased with the few rubles they possessed were those substances that could be resold on the Russian black market at home. It became quite evident that they were more interested in what they could buy in the few shops in Kirkenes than in the size of their catch of fish. In groups of three, they would come ashore while their vessels received attention, the unshaven sailors ignoring language difficulties to buy and to haul back to their ships American tobacco products, silk underwear, and perfumes. An underground barter system developed, exchanging codfish in bulk quantities for the goods produced by the countries of the West. The Norwegian vendors immediately converted the fish into the delivery system going to the markets of the European cities. When the cod was not the venue of exchange, four-ounce tins of caviar became the currency of value. From out of the frozen seas of the Arctic Ocean, a commercial trade arose not seen since the days of the nineteenth-century pomor commerce.

The business people of Kirkenes quickly accommodated to the new market. For a village of approximately five thousand people, the amount of trade far surpassed the average per capita krona volume. The drydock facility at the port was upgraded to give the full services needed by the Russian fleet. The runway at the airfield was lengthened to serve three round-trip jet flights daily. Braathens and SAS airlines brought in 727s. At the airfield, buses met the planes. Food services and refueling personnel were hired. Tourist facilities meant increased business for the two hotels. As the need arose even tours were organized to the old border outposts, to the abandoned nickel mines, to the checkpoints at Boris Gleb, and to the ancient narrow gauge railroad. The wharf warehouse of Nor-Cargo was expanded and was modernized. Kirkenes was the beneficiary of this invisible life.

Although the protein of the codfish was a vital item to the Russian diet, there was no way the tonnage of fish could be adequately policed until it arrived at the home ports of the Russian fishing boats. Along the arctic rim, the Norwegian ports, Honningsvaag, Mehamn, Berlevag, Batsfjord, Vardo, and Kirkenes served as emergency stops for ship repair and for the clandestine activity for the Russian crews.

How much below the surface did the corruption invade? Nothing was written. The press was far removed. Prying television cameras never ventured into the far north. Only a few contact points had to be cemented through the system. Fish was the visible source of the hard currency. Still, this was purely the surface of the scheme. In full reality the Russian mafia used the system to deliver hard drugs, primarily cocaine, into Europe.

Filets of cod were packed in vinyl plastic. The plastic was packed into cardboard boxes averaging about forty pounds. Loaded by forklifts into the hull of coastal freighters, the fish was transported to Bergen, Norway, for airlift transport overnight by refrigerated 747s to Rome, Italy. Utilizing this system, similar packets of powdered drugs implanted in plastic containers were placed in the same-size cardboard boxes and the packets were transshipped. Tons of cod disguised the suggestion of cocaine. An enormous load of cod could easily hide bulk drugs. Never did every shipment of fish include drugs. Only the contact people in the Norwegian north and the fish mongers at the final destination in Rome had knowledge of the container numbers bearing the illegal product. In Italy the hard drugs were sold, the money was laundered, and the Russian mafia gathered the riches. The less people involved in the transfer, the less chance there was for the breakdown of the line. With few men involved in the drug marketing, any violation would give immediate information as to the weak link.

Police emphasis was always centered on drug entrance coming into Europe from the south, from Turkey through the Bosphorus, from Syrian avenues, or from the ports of the Libyan coastline. Attention was paid to Algerian and to Tunisian sources. However, absolutely no reason existed for drug penetration to be anticipated from the arctic. Any drug discovery in Italy would certainly not focus the limelight on Norway.

It is amazing what little boys between the ages of six and of sixteen learn in small villages throughout the world. This is especially true in a place as remote as Kirkenes. Ice and darkness abound through the winter months, when these boys stir about on bicycles, on foot, and on sleds. When the warmer weather finally returns, it is as if all that energy has been pent up, only to explode in volcanic proportions.

On the gravel and asphalt roads of Kirkenes in the long hours of daylight during the spring and the summer months, very little happened that did not attract my attention. As one of the hometown boys, I, Ivar Enge, roamed with the freedom of the wind. The people of the town knew me. Even the dogs did not bark when I rode past them on my bicycle. It was as if I was so commonplace that I had become almost invisible. This was good and this was bad.

I knew every pothole in the roads. I understood when each family ate their meals. Every article of new clothing that was purchased fell under my watchful gaze. Every hairstyle alteration on the girls came under my approving eye. As the children grew, I had full knowledge as to which boy could throw a stone the greatest distance. In my mind, I had all the hounds in Kirkenes ranked according to fighting ability. In turn, I felt that I had appraisal of which dog enjoyed having his ear scratched. When hungry I had full knowledge which farmhouse kitchen would reward the bearer of a bunch of wildflowers with some recently baked delicacy.

Kirkenes was mine. I had conquered it by right of possession. Time gave me right of passage over any ground. As the puffin soars at will, I was at liberty. As long as I behaved within the bounds of decency, I had no leash. Leki and my mother were my sole restrictions. Even dear Leki would sometimes look away when I made an error. The three-year difference in our ages made for a closeness. Yet, Leki's thoughtfulness could be tested when my transgressions became major.

Growing up together, I treated Leki with utmost respect. As she developed body changes, as she attracted the attention of boys, and as she gave out the silent signals to those young men she liked, I maintained total discretion. Rarely did she confide in me her private thoughts, but I felt like I understood them anyway. I told her plainly if I felt like she should avoid certain boys. She usually listened attentively and valued my words. Occupying the ground floor with my mother, with me sleeping in the upstairs, we were a united family.

Leki had a unique ability to syphon off the uncomfortable events she caught me in, to either forget them, or to not tell my mother. I do not mean to imply that she would completely protect me, but she had good judgment.

On one instance Leki caught me out on the airport road in the stave, abandoned shack with one of the village girls. With the busty girl's blouse totally open, I was enjoying myself so much that neither of us heard Leki's bicycle approach. In a state of complete embarrassment, Leki seemed to feel my discomfort.

Later at home, Leki put her arm around my shoulders and said, "Ivar, you are only normal."

That was all that was ever said about the event. She had the gift of evaluating the important and weeding out the unimportant. She had the typical Scandinavian attitude about my pubescence.

We rarely spoke about Leki's mother's death. Of course when it did come up, the grief was still there. However, at no time did I ever disclose what I had seen in the dim light near the statue. I knew that I had to be very certain of the time and of the place. Only when I was dealing from a situation of complete strength could I use my memory of that night. In the meantime, my mother, Leki, and I continued our valiant struggle for the necessities of life.

On one occasion, possibly in a moment of weakness, my mother spoke to Leki and to me about a certain man whom she sensed wanted to show her some attention. At that time both Leki and I were old enough not to feel this as a threat to our lives. We were in agreement that my mother should go along with his actions if mother wished.

With that, my mother said, "Oh, no. I am too old for that. I have responsibility here enough with you two. I refuse to take on more."

At least in commenting on this event, a private part of her world, she brought us into her thoughts, letting us know that she was human. We admired her sacrifice in doing all she did to raise us. Very little did she allocate for her own pleasures. Of course, one could ask what luxuries were required in Kirkenes. Nevertheless, we understood what she had achieved.

Her life centered around our modest house, the work at the Rica Hotel, the Lutheran church, our school, and the infrequent ladies' informal discussion groups. Shopping took minimal time as the concentration of stores all fell in the same row. Clothing was all the same type—simple, basic, and warm. Like all the inhabitants of northern Norway and of comparable frigid regions, fashion gave way to warmth and to comfort. In a small square plot of ground behind the hotel, my mother continued to plant some flowers, anticipating the enjoyment of color. Never did these blooms flourish. In a way the flowers or the lack thereof bespoke much of the existence in that climate. It was good to hope, although never did the expectations in life fully blossom.

To break the boredom in Kirkenes, occasionally inhabitants would wander down to the Nor-Cargo warehouse and stand in the lee of its sides, expecting the arrival of the coastal steamer. Docking at 11:30 A.M. each morning and leaving promptly at 1 P.M., the ship signified to the onlooker that one contact with the outside world, that one vital link with civilization. Watching the forklifts unload the supplies, the people intently assessed what was new. Almost all of the time they were sorely disappointed. The unloaded freight was a repetition of what was utilized for previous months on end. In like manner, the material the two forklifts took into the hull of the freighters was the same fish products coming out of Finmark province. Packaged securely in containers designed to cushion against shock, then lined in wooden crates, the townspeople easily recognized what was hidden in the pallets going into the vessels. The activities were truly boring, except that there was nothing else moving in town.

Over in the drydock yard at the headwater of the fjord, ship repair continued all the year. However, there was nothing there for the onlooker to watch. The airstrip was a full three kilometers out of town. Although not far, in the unpredictable arctic the three kilometers could leave one stranded with the onslaught of a sudden storm. Even if the weather were good, the arrival of a jet airplane happened so quickly that there was not much to see. Most of the passengers, who were local, were recognized. Newcomers were sparse. Almost all tourists were only going into town, to await the arrival of the next southbound freighter.

I understood that even I, Ivar Enge, blended into the mist of the usual, losing my form and my identify. I felt that eventually I would be absorbed into this abyss of ice, frozen into eternity, when all the energies of adolescence were rising. However, this ability to assimilate into the environment, combined with the silence of travel by bicycle, gave me the ability to roam far and wide, to be on the scene before people were aware of my presence, and to see many things that were not necessarily meant for my eyes. I did not purposely wish to invade on others' privacy; it just happened. The smallness of the community, the fact that I knew everybody, and the fact that I understood what everybody should be doing, made me acutely sensitive when an action was out of the ordinary.

This was the case early one morning when I saw Kirkenes' lone lawman at the pallet of fish outside the Nor-Cargo wharf. Working through a gap in the vinyl covering of the container, he removed a small packet and inserted an equal size and similar mass into the vacated cavity. As he smoothed the hole in the plastic, I ducked around the corner of the building and I rode off down the road to the schoolhouse. From time to time during the day, I pondered over this strange activity. Like the time when I saw the outline of the woman's form being carried by the policeman, like the time when Leki saw me fondling the girl's breasts, like the many times when I wanted to quiz my mother about my father, it seemed to be a Scandinavian trait to mentally file away the information. Even at age sixteen, I had the arctic instincts to not act hastily until demand forced an action. Whether the cold climate gives this trait to the Norse attitude or whether it is genetically inherited by my people, I do not know. But, it seems to be an integral part of my behavior.

To substitute one packet of fish for another bundle did not make sense, so I just filed what I had seen away in my memory. How could I reach a judgment, when all I had seen was a strange sighting?

Rather than dwell on minute occurrences, I was more concerned with the rapid approaching time of scholastic exams. Realizing that further education was totally determined in Norway by a system designed to pick out the promising youngsters for higher schooling, I was determined to show well on the examinations. Only by a demonstration of prowess could I alter my entire future. If I could secure appointment to a university, I would relieve my mother of a burden, I would make the cramped housing situation less for my mother and for Leki, I would increase my chances for the future, and I would get to leave Kirkenes. This thought was so dominant that nothing else seemed to matter. I refused to let myself think of alternative paths.

As I grow, living upstairs appears to cramp not just me, but to cause the entire family to be on edge. Leki is still at home. She has little ambition to strike out for herself. To me, her sole view of the future is to marry a local Norwegian lad, to settle down, and to have a house full of babies. It sounds as if I am pulling Leki down. I am not. I am only trying to describe what I think Leki wants for her future. Leki is magnificent in that she enjoys more than her share of the household duties. One of her hobbies is cooking. She sews and mends. Having a strong and well shaped body, Leki can participate in all of the outdoor activities. Her movements do not hide a grace that projects beauty of function. With a joyous laughter, she attracts many of the young men. It is this total package that disgusts me when I want more for Leki than what she seems to be willing to settle on as companions. All of the superior boys have gone off to university training in southern Norway. Leki is left with the culls. What troubles me, I feel that Leki is satisfied with these second category companions. Although I am not her true brother, and although I am three years younger, I want better for Leki than she is willing to accept.

Another reason I want to leave Kirkenes is to relieve my mother of the financial drain. I feel that in a university setting I could work part-time, support myself with the federal subsidy, thereby giving my mother more cash. Of course, she would miss me and I would miss her. That is only natural. But, I feel that is purely the natural evolution of growth.

To not kid myself with attempts to rationalize out my desires, now that I am sixteen years old, I want to see more of the world than Kirkenes. I want to be in a place where it is not completely dark three months of the year. I want to see people that I do not know by name. I want to hear a dog bark at me because he does not know me. Every dog in Kirkenes I have scratched behind the ear. I want to see girls that I have not grown up with, living side by side all my life. I want to experience the mystery of a girl whose every secret I do not know. I want to go into a store that does not face the paved square of Kirkenes. I want the learning experience of seeing God's creation. I thank God, as Ivar, Takk Gud, as Ivar Enge; I realize my blessings. I am not satisfied with being the biblical buried talent. I want to compound my gifts, my days, and my energies.

As I rethink all of my wants, I am not ashamed.

Continuously ringing in my ears are Leki's words, "Ivar, you are only normal."

Just as I want to get away from Kirkenes, the other side of me wants to return after a period of development. Following the growth experience of university, I would like somehow to be involved in the nurturing and in the husbanding of the enormous potential for growth in the northern provinces of Norway. With weather as the constant hindrance, that portion of Norway from Tromso to Kirkenes has not benefited from the cultivation of modern civilization. The frozen tundra does not limit mankind from fully employing electronics, from utilization of jet aviation, from the geo-satellite positioning in navigation, and in the exploitation of the Arctic Ocean. The treacherous demand for exactness because of the cold teaches one slowness to eliminate harsh errors through rash decisions. Having been raised in the arctic environment, I think I possess the inborn trait of deliberate calculation. I am not alone in having that gift, for I think it is most common in the Viking progeny.

Looking back on my prior fifteen years, I realize I have in my subconscious mind demonstrated this trait on key occasions. Being able to file away the image of Mrs. Knutson's body, placing on hold the act of the policeman substituting the box in the fish pallet, and harnessing pent-up emotions of adolescence when village girls were plying their bodies to me, all enable me to know myself. It is not that I am so insecure that I can not talk with my mother or with someone in the role of a mentor. I work best as a lone individual, realizing that in some issues, haste can be detrimental. When I see the enormous results of glacial power, I understand how the earth was dented by an infinitely slow force of ice. The crushing momentum of the glacier does things unrecognized by the eye of man with his short life span. Yet, the world senses the silent authority. To me, the Norwegian has assimilated this characteristic into his own personality. I am proud when I recognize that I have this trait.

My glaring weakness is my inexperience. Without innumerable daily requirements to exercise judgment, I understand I do not possess the common street knowledge to render decisions. In my comfortable surroundings of Finmark province, I do not feel comfortable seeing the different shades of black changing to white. Blended with human guile, I know that I can be manipulated by evil. All of these skills are due to my lack of human contact. I trust that over time in a university setting that I can acquire the ability to judge other human beings, to see through their motives, and to foresee satanic forces.

All of these thoughts, at age sixteen, trouble me as I introspectively assess my future.

CHAPTER FIVE

He that is slow to anger
is better than the mighty;
and he that ruleth his spirit than
he that taketh a city.

—Proverbs 16:32—

THE WINTER NIGHT, THE CONSTANT COLD, THE EVER-PRESENT wind all contributed to the crisp appearance of the Christmas lights decorating the outsides of the homes in the town of Kirkenes. Very few souls ventured outside with the temperatures staying below freezing. Snow mixed with slush covered the streets. The dogs were indoors. No bird calls were heard. Only the infrequent vehicle engine racket penetrated the air.

I meditated on this being my last Christmas at home before going away to school. Sadness smothered the joyous season. I wanted my mother to be happy. Still, I could sense her moodiness. She went through all the motions, but she did not give off the usual energy. The work at the hotel was virtually nonexistent this time of year. Of course, she had to show up for work at the usual hours, but there was nothing to do.

Leki filled the vacuum. With a vigor exhibited by youth, she went from house, to church, to the stores, and to the village pageants. She filled the small house with the smells of freshly baked sweets. Children of the neighborhood were entertained. Leki was keenly involved in the youth productions presented at the church.

For a long time I had tried to draw a link between Mrs. Knutson's death and the strange sight of the village policeman switching cardboard boxes in the pallet of fish waiting in the cold atmosphere of the dock. The two events were widely separated in time. However, the uniformed man was the common denominator in both. Maybe I was jumping to

27

conclusions that had no valid meaning. Nevertheless, I wanted to know. I had to devise some method to answer the question without hurting anyone, without pointing the finger at me, and without making my mother and Leki being cast into an uncomfortable situation.

For a long time I had been thinking about a scheme. During this pre-Christmas season, I would be home for the last time, if I passed my university exams. If nothing were answered as a result of my caper, the only cost would be the value of a box of codfish. Surely, I could not see how any solution would come about because of my adventure. However, in carrying out my stunt, possibly I would have an indicator that the two events were interlinked.

I began a routine bicycle ride, in spite of the weather. To set no precedent, I would ride from home either after dinner or early in the morning. Wrapped up in heavy clothes, my route first went primarily downhill, down past the isolated coffee shop on the gravel road to the Nor-Cargo warehouse, around the storage barn along the dock, and back into town along the waterfront road. Sometimes along this route I paused at the coffee shop to lean my bicycle against the side wall of the shop, walking the rest of the way around the warehouse. Other times I rode the bicycle the entire circle around the Nor-Cargo metal building. Each time around the warehouse I paid particular attention to the pallets containing fish, focusing my inspection without pausing to the plastic drawn over the entire pallet. Having reached the coffee shop, if I were on foot, I would get back on my bicycle and resume my route. If I had ridden around the dock, I paid particular attention to the tire marks left by my bicycle. If I walked that segment of the route, I looked back to inspect my boot prints. In the heavy snow and slush I came to understand how to disguise my tracks. If there had been a slit in the plastic enveloping the fish pallets, I tried to make a mental note as to where the opening had been made, at what height, at what corner, and on what daily or weekly basis.

As I made my rides around the waterfront road, when reaching the church cemetery, I would dismount and I would walk my bicycle up the steep incline through the grave sites to the plaza around the church that fronts onto the village square. This walk, pushing my bicycle, made complete sense because it was the shortest way around an otherwise steep hill. From that point I resumed my ride. In the evenings I rode home. In the mornings I rode to the schoolhouse. The entire circuit normally took me between seven and fifteen minutes, somewhat dependent on the level of snow and the wind direction along the waterfront road.

In the minds of my mother and Leki, along with any in the village who saw my rides, I wanted to establish that this was my usual habit. I wanted them to think that Ivar was taking his routine form of exercise. To cap off the image, I occasionally stopped to inspect my sports watch on my wrist. Putting a variable into the system, I made the bicycle ride sometimes in the evening, sometimes in the mornings, but both times there was no daylight.

Over a month passed before I assumed that there was no set pattern to the slit in the plastic covering of the fish crates. However, the artificial openings were always at shoulder level. As hard as I thought, I could not imagine what was going on with the substitution of one box for another similar box by the constable. The senselessness only compounded the suspicion. I knew that he would not be stealing cod. In Norway that would be like robbery at the ice plant. Neither could I get any idea what was in the cardboard box he was sending in the fish container.

My only answer was to obtain a cardboard box the same size. That posed no problem whatsoever. Not knowing the weight, I determined that I would have my similar box filled with the lightweight styrofoam peanuts. I did not want to have the box at home. I could not store it in the hollows of the caves near the Soviet soldier's statue on the hill for fear that the young children of the village would get into its contents as a plaything. I finally deemed that I could store it one day in advance in the dump for the garbage on the side of the coffee shop. By placing a piece of plastic over the box to protect it from the weather, from the snow and ice, it would not cast any suspicion. As part of my routine I could quickly work a second substitution on the box left by the policeman. In every case, I had never seen the policeman stay around the wharf. The position of the fish pallets was not visible except from the water of the fjord. Hence, no eyes in the village could see the transfer. What had protected the policeman from being seen, the sheltered position would also make my transfer invisible.

I had no idea what was in the container I would be removing. I had no idea as to its weight. If heavy, I could not guarantee that I could balance it on my bicycle as I made my getaway. Realizing that my first problem would be weight, if I could not manage it, I would have to deposit it in the deepest part of the dockside fjord, hopefully in a shredded or dismembered condition. If it were light in weight, I planned to ride with the box on my handlebars to the church cemetery. At that point, I could pause long enough to inspect the contents. Based on the material, I would have to make an immediate decision, to either drop it in a watery grave along the rocks bordering the waterfront, or to place the contents in a quickly devised shallow hole in the graveyard. Soon my attention centered on paying attention to areas where there was some disturbed moss overlying the scanty topsoil in the cemetery.

I could see no other way. I knew that a sixteen-year-old boy had no alternative in confronting the one authoritative figure in Kirkenes. Not knowing the contents of the box, I understood that my strength resided in my being ultimately patient. After I had performed my mission, I had only to wait. If nothing came of it, I could mark my scheme up to juvenile pranks. Before going any further, I wanted to run this entire crazy act through my mind. It had been many years since Mrs. Knutson had died. Was I a total fool? Still, I felt a gnawing allegiance to Leki.

I ran the worst possible scenarios through my mind. I could abort the mission at any time, even during the bicycle ride. It would only last fifteen minutes or so. If caught in the act, it would be petty thievery. As a juvenile, I would get a slap on the wrist. It would not jeopardize my going to a university. My mother and Leki would gasp at this out of character behavior on my part. Nevertheless, they would get over it. If my act came to the attention of the policeman, he would be forced into ignoring the situation rather than run the risk of exposing himself if he were truly doing something in a criminal way.

Do I do it?

The pragmatism of the Nordic consumed my thoughts. With the passage of the years since the death of Leki's mother, I wondered if I were carrying this whole idea to ridiculous extremes. Using Old Testament patience, I pondered if it were morally correct to do an evil deed, however small, if the consequences possibly could shed some light on a woman's unsolved death. Over all these years I have held a secret grudge that the policeman was implicated. What have I to assume that substituting one box of fish for another box is suspicious? Even if I obtained an answer, what was I to do with any information?

In my daydreams I pictured myself in ancient Athens. Sitting on the hard granite steps under an olive tree absorbing the logic of a Socrates, I wrestled with the facts. Was this entire outline a fantasy? Part of the puzzle was the missing item. I did not know what I was seeking.

Resting in the quiet of my upstairs bed, I became fixed on that one big question. Sin is evil, measured by any method of calculation. To rationalize out of the dilemma by claiming that the sin was small or by thinking that I had never done anything like that before was wrong. That thought was perfectly clear. Before falling asleep, I made a conscious effort to control my emotions.

The constable had been functioning in Kirkenes for years. His wife died ten years ago. His children were grown and had moved to Oslo. Rarely had there been any strife in Kirkenes. He had certainly not done anything to harm me or my mother. If I had an ulterior motive to dislike him, I was unable to bring it up in my mental distress.

I gained no answers before falling asleep.

At least I had the strength to discipline my spirit. I did nothing hastily.

I fell into sleep, dreaming of the massive forces of slow moving glaciers leaving behind craters in granite.

With January came more darkness, more cold, more snow, more wind, but also the university examinations. I think I did fairly well. However, I will not receive the results until early March. The popularity of the winter sport season around Oslo does not extend up to Kirkenes. Here it is pure survival. One does not ski nor ice skate for sport. A person thinks about how to stay indoors.

Although the weather curtailed my daily trips, I still made the occasional trip to the Nor-Cargo docks. Each time I made the rounds I saw with increasing frequency the telltale slit in the plastic covering of the fish pallets. Finally, I decided that I had to do the deed if I were ever going to try for answers.

First, the cardboard box containing the peanut-sized styrofoam pellets was dropped on the trash pile on the side of the now-closed coffeehouse. I laid over the box a small piece of vinyl, tucked on all sides, to protect it from the elements. This was all placed on my way to school. Later that evening, after dinner while Leki and my mother were cleaning the kitchen, I went out on my bicycle.

Leki exclaimed, "Ivar, you are completely crazy to go out on nights like this."

Mother retorted, "Oh, let him go. He will sleep better."

These comments were in no way out of the ordinary. Their thought processes were just what I would have expected. Their weight carried no real concern nor worry.

Riding to the coffee shop, I decided to lean the bicycle against the side wall and to make the rest of the way on foot, carrying the box in my arms. This would enable me to keep a sharp outlook around me. In actuality, it was so dark, it made little difference. As I rounded the corner of the warehouse I could not make out the tear in the plastic covering. Only when I was within six paces could I see the vertical slip. After placing the box I was bringing with me flat in the snow, I reached into the opening to withdraw the nearest package. It was far too heavy to remove with ease. At this point, panic struck my thought process. I knew that I could not speedily remove it nor carry it with me on the bicycle.

My first impulse was to abort the whole plan.

Then it dawned on me to make an opening vertically in the corner of the box to check the contents. To my surprise, on the inside was another layer of plastic. It was so dark that there was no way that I could make out the inside contents. I slit the box horizontally and I found that I could squeeze out the plastic bag resting in that corner. The inner bag had an amorphous content that took on any shape except for the tightness of the restraining plastic. Knowing that it was futile to try to remove the entire box, I revolved it around until the opening I had caused was on the back and inner side adjacent to the interior boxes. Satisfied that it was in no way visible, I heaved my own box of styrofoam pellets into the fjord's water next to the dock. Whether that box floated or was blown away by the wind, I did not care.

Picking up the stolen plastic package, I swiftly walked to my bicycle leaning against the coffeehouse wall. In the pitch black darkness, I could see nothing stirring. In my ride around the waterfront road, fired by the burst of adrenaline in my system, I made record time to the churchyard cemetery. As my usual, I dismounted the bicycle, pushed it up the incline through the gravestones, and stopped long enough to check the contents of my purloined bag. Realizing that in the dense darkness in the lee of the church building I could see nothing, I edged to the corner of the sanctuary. With a bare minimum of light coming from the streetlamps of the town square, I opened the malleable exterior. Out poured a powdery substance that I thought might have been white, but I was not certain. The fine matter blew out in the wind scattering over the moss and mold covering the ground between the headstones. I quickly surmised that the combination of wind and of ground moisture would dissipate the evidence of the powder I had spilled on the ground. Touching my finger to the substance, and bringing it to my nose, I detected no odor. Putting my finger gently to the tip of my tongue, I could elicit no taste. Satisfied that I was frustrated and had nothing more to learn, I shook the entire fine powder into the wind. The swirls lasted on the stiff arctic breeze but a moment. It was so rapidly destroyed that I knew none of the cloud had gotten on my clothing. In a gust of wind I released the light plastic bag. It disappeared immediately upwards into the enveloping darkness.

The rest of the bicycle ride back home was made in a blur of mixed emotions. On one hand, I was frustrated to not get an answer. I do not know what I expected, but I had not planned this. I was confused by my contrary feelings of relief.

My months of thought had been spent on a frigid ride in the dark, on releasing an amorphous powder into the wind, and on solving nothing.

CHAPTER SIX

৵৸

A stone statue and a dead man
do not speak.

—Ancient proverb—

I HAD SETTLED INTO THE NORGES TEKNISKE HOYSKOLE (University of Trondheim). My departure from Kirkenes was greeted by tears from my mother. Of course, she was overjoyed that I had been accepted, especially with the help of grants. She wanted the opportunities that the education would give me. Nevertheless, it is every mother's dread when a child departs the nest. It is the symbolic cutting of the umbilical cord, the fledgling bird leaving the tree, the roaming young stallion separating himself from the herd. It is a final act of growth, enacted in the moment of departure, and yet, spread over weeks of anticipation and of planning.

Leki's reaction was one of resignation, that although she was older, her desires were tied to the home. She sincerely understood that her deep-down desires were to have a husband, a home, and children. Her fantasies were about the images of curtains in the windows, of the arrangement of her stove and countertops, about the picket fence lining the boundaries of a little yard, and her ability to sew during the long winter nights. Leki firmly voiced how she would miss me. But, in the next breath she would joke about the freedom she would have because of not having to babysit with her little brother. Leki's opinions were never complex; she said what she thought, and she was predictable. I loved her dearly and thought of her as my sister.

Leki's final question to me was, "Can I have your upstairs bed, may I throw out your old junk, and may I clean the mausoleum you have lived in over all these past years?"

I answered, "Do whatever makes you happy."

I said that with a smile on my face. I wanted my mother and Leki to see my grin. But, inwardly, I experienced a little pain. I recognized the finality of the moment.

Like all students, I did not know exactly what to expect from university life. Small details of day by day living went by unnoticed. My biggest adjustment was in the application of the hours into a regimen allocated to study, segmented by periods devoted to the logistics of everyday living. I found this freedom invigorating. It was as if the rigors of the Arctic had tempered me with the inborn discipline to adapt.

Trondheim, Norway's first capital, is a city of 140,000 inhabitants. Originally named Nidaros, the town grew at the junction of the river, Nid, with the fertile plains lining the Trondheims Fjord. After the time of the Vikings, by the 1100s Trondheim became the seat of the archbishop. Nidaros Cathedral is now one of northern Europe's most revered Gothic memorials. The technical school and research institute is the largest university north of Bergen.

Of importance to me in selecting Trondheim for my university training, it is the city having a good college closest to Kirkenes. Having a different climate, even Trondheim is distant to my home area of Finmark. Trondheim has a jet airport with several daily flights to Kirkenes. Every day the coastal express steamship freighters leave, going both northbound and southbound between Trondheim and Kirkenes. Although the fare by ship is cheaper than by jet, the voyage is a full four days each way. Hence, I could get back to Kirkenes easily when necessary.

Trondheim is considered to be located in middle Norway. Tempered by the waters of the North Sea, Trondheim is considerably warmer than my home. Located south of the Arctic Circle, the soil is rich. The farms lining the fjord are green much of the year. Vegetables and meats locally produced supply the markets. Light industry, transport, and fishing share the work of the people along with education.

Unlike Kirkenes where I recognized everybody, one could get lost among all the people in Trondheim. Although the city enveloped a large area, I quickly learned my way around. Because of the fixed points, the fjord, the harbor, and the surrounding hills, I had my location fixed at all times. With a wonderful transportation system, I could maneuver easily. In spite of the hills, I determined that I could use my bicycle, which I left in Kirkenes. Rather than wait on trying to bring the bicycle by ship when I was next in Kirkenes, I secured a used cycle which was in good shape.

With my mother's experience in the Rica Hotel, I realized that with discipline I could study and at the same time do part-time work at the front desk of a large downtown hotel. When I specifically requested work on the 8 P.M. to midnight shift, I was hired on the spot. As it turned out, at the dinner hour and afterwards, one had very little to do at the reception counter. Unlike at the Rica, the telephones were all automatic. All of the passenger-carrying freighters and the ferryboats became inactive. Some aircraft passengers arrived by taxi late, but they came in a bunch centered around the time of jet landings. In the meantime, most of the time I had a textbook in front of my face.

The part-time job eliminated much of the socializing. After classes, labs, and study time, I needed to run my errands. Contrary to the sometimes boredom of Kirkenes, I found my situation to be wonderful.

Like in all parts of the world, alcohol, drugs, dance clubs, and "generally hanging out" were present in Trondheim. Nevertheless, I assume it is on a much smaller scale than in larger cities where the temperature is warmer and the students have more wealth. In any event, these vices did not tempt me. My only real vice was the number of good looking girls. Whereas in Kirkenes I had grown up with them all, I knew all of their peculiarities, and familiarity soured many potential alliances. Here in Trondheim the barnyard was full of chicks.

I truly was Ivar, Takk Gud. I thanked God that I had been given the opportunity to better myself.

In my gratefulness to God, I understood that my evaluation of my situation could not be calculated in terms of money, in terms of future wealth, nor in terms of material things in life. I was grateful for life. I had a mother who had given me love. With much sacrifice I had been presented with an upbringing that differentiated right from wrong. I was taught and had accepted a faith in Almighty God. Part of that faith was in the realization that the world was formed by God, even the frozen tundra of the Arctic, and that all people were created with the opportunity to accept God. I had these thoughts in concrete in my mind, without the benefit of university training.

Early in the school year I was asked the question many times, "What field of study, what major department, what type of profession do you want to pursue?"

I felt that it was too early to narrow my sights on any one field. I favored general arts and sciences. Nevertheless, my pragmatism told me that electrical engineering would be a valuable commodity in the job market. I was interested in the environmental aspect of the arctic region. Because of the influence of Kirkenes on me, I had a keen eye on transportation and on tourism in the far north. It was obvious that the present was no time to concentrate my thoughts and my efforts. My interests were too wide.

Christmas was the first break in the school year. Landing at the Kirkenes airfield gave me the feeling of the prodigal son returning. In a way, I felt guilty of having the experience of my Trondheim stay, a happening that very few people in Kirkenes had enjoyed. I did not feel better than them. Nor did I feel superior to them. I was in awe that I was chosen. In a mood of humbleness I was returning to my surroundings. Both my mother and Leki were waiting at the airfield. Having no need, we had never owned an automobile. That time of year, in the total darkness, we enjoyed the taxi ride to our home. I teased Leki about her having to temporarily give me back my upstairs bed.

My mother said that the only major change in Kirkenes since I left was the week-long absence of the town constable. He had given no notification about his sudden unannounced departure. No one at the two points of departure, the airfield and the ticketing office of the coastal express steamship, had any record of his leaving. The only other method of departure would have been by road southward in the direction of Karasjok. No monitoring of this avenue was possible. No townspeople had been told that he had plans to leave by fishing vessel. The sole ships that would depart without returning would be the itinerant Russian fishing trawlers. In the period in question, there were no ships to come out of the drydock repair and maintenance facility. For him to leave without official notification was most unusual.

The man had served Kirkenes in the capacity of policeman for many years. My mother was quite upset over this disturbing event.

Never had I voiced what I had seen many years ago at the statue of the Soviet soldier. Nor did I comment on the episode of the package substitution at the fishing pallet nor of my later involvement in robbing a sample out of the corner of the crate. I planned to keep quiet about my own thoughts, especially since those thoughts did not seem interrelated. I guess my stoic Nordic trait about not speaking without a definite purpose continued.

During my short Christmas stay in Kirkenes, my mother commented further about the policeman.

"Do you remember several years ago when I was talking to you and to Leki about a man in Kirkenes who was giving off signals that he possibly wanted to show me some attention? Both of you urged me to follow my heart. At the time, my response was that I was not in the mood for other problems. That man was the constable."

While I was surprised by her statement, it explained why she was so agitated by his disappearance. I had no idea that the policeman was looked on by my mother as a potential suitor.

During the short interval while I was home in Kirkenes, outside law enforcement officials arrived in Finmark to start an official inquiry. I had no idea that one person's absence would trigger an investigation from the national authorities. Those people interviewed did not include me. I am not certain I would have brought up anyway what I felt were uncertain, misleading, and purposeless sightings. I had no proof that what I had seen bore any importance. Those things I had seen many months and years ago I could not collaborate anyhow. It was my decision not to volunteer any additional facts to the investigating team. It did not dawn on me that if I spilled all I knew, then it would be their determination as to whether it was important or not. To bring up my knowledge would disclose what I had done in robbing the plastic package from the crate of fish. After all, the man was only missing. I felt that he would eventually show up anyway.

Later, I would learn that I was the one who did not know all the facts.

My trip back to Trondheim was like a journey through an endless tunnel of time, from an environment frozen in actuality, into the world of modern civilization. On my first trip to Trondheim I was so tense that my eyes did not see the magnificent transition. This time I could appreciate the enormous change the trip south the Arctic Circle demonstrated. Even in the same country, Norway, it is evident that the cold controls man and his existence. In Kirkenes, one's energy is channeled into pure survival. In Trondheim, that energy is sufficient to allow some left over for the enjoyment of arts and of crafts. Attention can be spread to music, to painting, to appreciation of architecture and home furnishing. The terrain in Kirkenes is granite outcropping, mixed with the occasional wet bog created by the gravitational effects of an ancient glacier. In Trondheim, the contrasting land is soil containing the minerals ground finely by retreating glaciers. The land along the

Trondheim Fjord has some of the most productive farms in all of Norway. Crops flooding the market permit mankind to vary his diet, transferring the energy of the land into quality of life.

These same positive elements in Trondheim have a relatively negative result in the activities of man. Whereas in Trondheim, man's hours can be filled to the maximum with matters of interest. In Kirkenes, those same hours have to be spent on more introspective meditation. One thinks longer before acting. The harsh elements cause one to weigh the necessity of every move. Consequently, the individual spends more of his time in deep thought. I feel that growing up in Kirkenes has caused me to blend this pensive attitude into the inner core of my personality. What appears to be stoicism is premeditative. What seems to be placid is actually mentally calculated, forged by a will tempered by the elements of the environment. What is deemed on the surface to be slow to react is truly a process whereby mistakes are eliminated in advance. I see myself in this light, effected by my growing up in Kirkenes.

And for this, I thank God. I am truly Ivar, Takk Gud.

In the middle of the winter I was glancing through a Trondheim newspaper. An article appeared mentioning an investigation taking place by the authorities in Oslo on the presence of drug traffic in Norway. One of the sentences told of the inquiry on Russian trans-shipment of cocaine from the Caucasus region across the USSR, exiting by White Sea ports, and laundered through Russian fishing trawlers into the west. One line in the article hit me between the eyes.

"A long-term policeman in Kirkenes is missing. No link has been proven between this man and the drug trade. However, an ongoing question is being thoroughly scrutinized."

This is all the newspaper placed in the article. It left me totally perplexed. I did not know what side of the law the central government officials suspected the lawman to be following. It only confirmed that the Kirkenes policeman was still missing. On one side it could be interpreted that the constable, working on the drug problem, had stumbled on to something. As a result of his knowing something, the Russian mafia had it set up that the policeman would be eliminated. The other way to interpret the newspaper article was that the lawman was working in collusion with the drug importers. Feeling the pressure of approaching apprehension, he could have fled. I could not reach any conclusion.

I thought about the question. I, certainly, did not want to telephone my mother. She may have known more than I did. But, if she did not, I did not want to bring up the tale.

I decided to place my curiosity on hold. Surely, something would come up later. My prior sightings of the policeman carrying Mrs. Knutson's body and of the transfer by the officer of the package in the fish container confused my thinking. I could draw no conclusions. However, my spine chilled when I assumed that the powder I had spread to the winds in the church graveyard was really a plastic container of cocaine.

If it were not cocaine, what was the fine powder?

If it was cocaine, could my petty thievery be classified as a major robbery both by the crime mob and by the Norwegian authorities? I wondered if my stealing the bag of drugs could have shortchanged the inventory at the downstream arrival site, thereby pointing the accusing finger directly at the only transferring link in the transportation system, namely the Kirkenes contact man—the policeman? If this were so, did the Russians kill him? I knew that there was an awful expanse of untra- versed Arctic water as a dumping site for a body. In the bitter cold, in the choppy waves, in the rocky coastline of the relatively uninhabited far north ocean, the chances of a body ever being discovered was remote.

If the scenario were drugs, as I suspected, what was my relatively innocent role? At this point, with the absence of in-depth information, I concluded that I should do nothing. As yet, other than my own chance glancing at the newspaper article, I was not involved, other than in the confusion of my own mind. Even then, I could not see my direct impli- cation. Unless, of course, one concludes that my thievery triggered the gangsters to act against the constable.

Falling back on my Nordic instincts, I decided to do nothing.

The dead of winter in Trondheim, dark around the clock, is not nearly as dreadful as the cold of Kirkenes. In Kirkenes there is nothing to do. In Trondheim, the city lights punctuate the darkness. The university activities give vent to the boredom of the cold. The winter sports organizations occupy the energies of the college students. Between my studies and my part-time job at the front desk at the hotel, I am forced to allocate my time wisely. On the few occasions when I need to get outdoors, I walk the paved sidewalks from the docks to the front of the hotel. When I leave my quarters, I can walk, delaying my evening meal to leftovers at the hotel before assuming my job at eight o'clock. The entire circuit is about a mile and a half. Coursing over several small bridges and running along the waterfront by the Nor-Cargo warehouses, I have time to feel the sting of the droplets of frigid water crashing against the rocks of the harbor. Even in the dark, I achieve a renewal of the spirit. I tend to think clearer. In the absence of daylight, my eyes are veiled from focusing on the scenery. Consequently, I am usually so deep in thought that I am in front of the hotel before I know it.

It was on one of these walks that I finally made up my mind to go to the proper authorities about the whole story pertaining to the Kirkenes policeman.

That same evening I was glancing at the Trondheim newspaper.

The lead story said, "Drug transfer scheme may have killed Kirkenes constable."

When I finished reading the short article, I had learned nothing new. Without giving facts, the newsprint merely stated that it was feared that there existed a relationship between the policeman and drug traffic. The sparse mention gave no details about what side of the law the constable was on, nor did it give specific data about him. This news article further set my mind on the decision to tell all I knew.

I felt uncomfortable about waiting until I was in Kirkenes. Also, I did not know who was filling the role of the village lawman. Once I had made up my mind, I thought that possibly the bigger town, Trondheim, would have a larger justice facility. I determined that the next afternoon I would walk into the local police office and ask to relate my full story. I hesitated to think about whether any officer would believe my story, whether any lawman would listen to a sixteen year old, and whether I would be implicated in any way by my stealing the packet of powder I had scattered to the wind in the cemetery.

Yet, I was resolved to tell all, if someone would listen.

In the central district of Trondheim, the main office of the police was located in a large stone building that was perfectly fitting for a city of its size. However, to me, coming from a small village, the structure was imposing. At the information desk, I asked to speak with any available investigator. The receptionist seemed somewhat perplexed by the unusual request. Momentarily, I could see that she was trying to categorize my inquiry. After a few seconds, she summoned a call to another person over her address system. With only a brief pause, a worker appeared who led me down a corridor to an elevator. On the third floor, she ushered me into a carpeted office dominated by a desk. To the side was a Norwegian flag on a floor mount. On the opposite side was another flag which I assumed to be the flag of either the district or the City of Trondheim.

The man in the dark suit rose. He motioned to one of the heavy chairs in front of his desk and said, "Please sit down. And, how can I help you?"

"I need to relate to someone about occurrences in my home village, Kirkenes, things I have seen that may be related to the disappearance of the town constable."

For several minutes, I outlined the general theme of my story. The investigator listened attentively. Then, he interrupted me.

He said, "What you are telling me is beyond the jurisdiction of this office. In fact, the information you know may have importance to intelligence officials in Oslo. I need to confer with them. It may take several days. I do not want you to speak of our meeting to anyone. Do not leave Trondheim. I will contact you, not in the name of my role as investigator, but strictly by my last name. The contact will be by telephone. You will not be embarassed by the visit of a uniformed officer. Ivar, I must ask you to subjugate your time and your studies, if you are requested to relate what you know and what you have seen."

I meekly answered, "I understand."

He lead me to the door and asked, "Do you think you can find your way out?"

I stated, "Yes, of course."

Four long days had passed since my session with the investigator. Nothing had happened. I had difficulty in keeping my mind on my

books. Time dragged. I did not sleep well. I do not remember the food
I had eaten. My social contacts had been virtually eliminated. My job at
the front desk at the hotel was continued. Overall, I had not varied my
daily pattern, except it was impossible to really study.

As I left work just after midnight, on the sidewalk steps of the hotel,
I recognized the investigator dressed in the long overcoat as he edged
over to me. I was totally surprised. At that hour of the night, there was
no traffic. No pedestrians could be seen in the entire block.

Without any comment of greeting, he instructed, "Follow me."

We crossed the street, going directly to the revolving door of the
competitor hotel. Quickly, I followed him past the reception desk to the
area before the elevator doors. Without any speech we went to a hotel
room. In my confusion I made no mental note of the room number.

Inside the room furnished as in any typical quarters, a large tray of
sandwiches and fruit sat on a coffee table. To the side rested the
ubiquitous coffee urn, with sugar packets and artificial cream. Standing
next to the window was a tall, rather young man. My investigator friend
introduced him to me. My mind was so dumfounded at this point that
I made no effort to either catch nor to remember the man's name.

The agent stated, "Look, it has been a long day. I have come from
Oslo. You have been up since early morning. I suggest you get some
sleep. There is a disposable razor and a new toothbrush in a kit in the
bathroom. Your room will be under close surveillance. Certainly, you are
not under arrest, but you are in far more danger than you realize. We
will get a fresh start tomorrow morning. You will be given a chance to
tell me all you know."

That is all he said.

With that, he abruptly left. He did not give me time to ask any questions.
My mind went over what I should do about my university commitments,
about my job across the street at the hotel front desk, and about what he
meant about me being in peril. How did he expect me to sleep? I
wandered about the room. Not fully understanding what I was doing, I
ate a sandwich. To my surprise, in the closet was a full set of clothing that
approximated my size. Even the pair of shoes was the size I wore.

By now, it was nearly 1:00 A.M. I thought about the agent's
mentioning that I needed to get some sleep. Taking heed, I took a
shower and went to bed. I do not know how long it was before I fell
asleep. However, the next thing I remember, I was startled by the sun's
rays and by the noise of traffic on the city streets.

I rushed through my morning preparations, ate some of the fruit on the table, and was brought into reality by a knock on the door. Before I could reach the door, the door opened and there stood the agent of the night before.

"Do not worry about all of your daily routines. Excuses have been adequately made in every situation. Shortly, governmental personnel will arrive to record all of our conversation. Is there anything you need? Fresh food and drink will be arriving in just a few minutes."

I replied, "I do not know of anything I need. I am just so totally confused. I initiated this request to give information. I did not know that it would lead to all of this. What is the eventual significance of all of this?"

The dark-suited agent said, "Please just accept this utmost security for your own benefit, for the benefit of your mother, and for Leki. We are prepared to record all of the information you can give us. Understand that we can not answer your questions. All I can relate to you is that you have stumbled upon something big, upon events that we have been shadowing for two years, and upon something that can suddenly blow up in our faces, and something that can kill you, your mother, and Leki. We will be the ones asking all the questions. We will limit our interrogations to today, get you back in your usual routine, and establish the rules for our future contact. Is that understood?"

He continued, "The less talk, the better. Dead men do not hear. Dead men do not speak. Thank God, Takk Gud, you are alive and can talk. Now, it is your time to tell all you have seen and have heard. We will take and will record all that you say."

As the machines began to record my voice, I said, "I am Ivar, Takk Gud, . . . I mean I am Ivar Enge."

CHAPTER SEVEN

Ice is tomorrow's water;
ice is tomorrow's life.

—Source in the Arctic, Unknown—

THE INTERVIEW WAS OVER. I HAD BEEN TOLD TO RESUME MY normal life. I was instructed to call only my agent contact in Oslo if I saw or learned anything I thought was in the least bit unusual. I was told that before the school year was completed I would be offered a job upstairs in the office of the Nor-Cargo warehouse on the pier in Kirkenes during the summer vacation. I was ordered to relate my experiences, my interrogation, with nobody, not even with my mother or with Leki.

The interview had ended abruptly. It seemed to me that the agent was satisfied with what I had told them. Nevertheless, I had a million questions. Yet, I was explicitly told that only they were the ones to ask questions.

The only hint, stressing the finality of the questioning period, was when the young agent smiled and said, "Consider yourself now to be part of the intelligence service of the Government of Norway."

At age sixteen, I had to self-impose clamps on my ego when I thought of myself as an agent of the national state. I could not talk with anybody. What was my role? What had I bungled into; who was involved in my awkward escapade? Had my interview with the intelligence official been a bust? Had it all been a joke? Had the agent's

45

final smile been a signal that I had paranoid delusions?

Still, he had freely given the name of Leki. He had indicated that he knew more of my home background than I surmised.

If I had truly nudged against a sensitive nerve, what did his comment encompass about my still being alive and able to talk?

As I mentally ran a time-retroactive analysis of the recent happenings, I came to the conclusion that I had to take every particle of the events with full seriousness.

My next conclusion was that at age sixteen, I was not ready for all of this.

My only recourse was to sink into the security of a normal university student's life. However, every day was filled with second thoughts, with feelings of looking over my shoulder, and with overanalysis of every event. I attempted to convince myself that in the university environment of Trondheim I was insulated from the dangers implied by the agent from Oslo. In my overanalysis, I talked myself into the possible belief that I could be the bait in a scheme that I knew nothing about and that I was a sacrificial lamb.

Of course, I was shocked by the government being aware of my mother and of Leki. I felt horrible when I drummed up thoughts that through my actions I could possibly have done something to endanger them. Not knowing the entire situation made it all the worse.

I could not help it. My mind had to skip from the various plots that might fit the big scenario. Foremost was the topic of drugs. It seemed obvious that murder had been blended into the picture. I had mentally eliminated the transshipment of radioactive nuclear waste. I could not see that fish could be the topic to gain hard currency. It did not fit that there was a move afoot for the Soviets to try further expansion into the vast area of the Arctic.

My mind settled on drugs. I was convinced that the powder I had scattered in the wind in the graveyard was really cocaine.

Going way back into my childhood, I wondered if Leki's mother had unearthed facts that necessitated her death. I could not help but mistrust the now-missing constable.

It was obvious to me that the Norwegian agent was placing me for the upcoming summer in the Nor-Cargo office over the wharf so that my eyes could spot anything out of the ordinary. I wished that I had an understanding about what I was going to be anticipating.

I guess that every university student, regardless of place or regardless of time, has a special place where he retires to think. When his mind needs a break from his studies, everyone finds a distinct refuge. I have two. One is on the grassy knoll on the ridge overlooking the harbor. Except for right in the middle of the day when tour buses unload noisy passengers, the site is vacant and is quiet. Even when the tourists are at the park, they do not tarry long. From this height, one can scan the entire city. The interisland ferryboats and the rapid hydrofoils leave beautiful wakes on the deep blue fjord. Only by listening closely can one pick up the distant sounds of the commuter trains or the city's vehicular traffic. Of course, the site can only be utilized comfortably in good weather. Realize, naturally, that the term "good weather" to a Norwegian is broad. In the winter, it is a favorite spot to start a descent into town on skis. If the temperature is not too cold, the aromas of the vegetation lend a pleasant symphony to the nose. On warm days when the wind is not like a robust zephyr, the ridge is my favorite spot for reading. I feel united with the outdoors, at peace with the world, in an environment where I thank God.

My second refuge is in the Nidaros Cathedral. Sitting in the middle of the central business area, one would tend to overlook the old church as a place of tranquillity. However, the enormous Gothic sanctuary is of such massive size that one can always find a site away from the nave that is isolated. Reading is limited only by the amount of sunlight under the high apse. Most of the time I can find an ideal location. I tune my mind out of the blurred sounds echoing off the stone walls. What sound waves that arrive at my ear are blended together, interpreted as the mystical murmurings of an ancient Gregorian chant. Surrounded by the tombs of Norway's legendary Viking chieftains, I feel at home. It is as if I blanket myself under the security of heroes of my ancestry. My spirit is invigorated. And I, then, can study in earnest.

The grey cathedral has been partially destroyed many times since its beginning in the middle of the twelfth century. The present restoration was begun in 1869. Today work continues. Limited by the skills of highly traditional craftsmen, construction is mixed with tourists, with the reverent, and with those like me. Only on special national holidays and on Sunday are formal church services held. All of the services are in the Norwegian Lutheran ritual. On the rare occasion when someone is playing the old organ, my concentration is not interrupted.

The straight-backed wooden chair only served to keep my mind alert. I had found an isolated spot away from the trail that tourists normally take going from the huge door to the altar. Light for reading was barely enough to read. The thick stone walls maintained the constant comfortable temperature. The smells were a blend of candles burning and with the blooms of the open-air flower market just outside the church. I had settled in for a respite that was never timed.

The girl had pushed an empty chair up close to mine before I really had taken register of her approach.

In the Norse language with a thick accent that I could not immediately place, she said, "I have seen you here before. Sometimes you read. Somedays you merely sit. I assume you are a student at the Norges Tekniske Hoyskole (University of Trondheim) by your books. My name is Victoria."

What I saw shook me out of my ethereal meditation. The girl, Victoria, was a leggy blond, wearing a grey turtleneck sweater, similar to the garb of the fishermen. This Nordic beauty was sufficient to send the hormones raging. I could not place the source of her accent, but it was definitely laced with somewhere foreign. I recognize the slight changes in the Norwegian language from the populous south to my home area in the frozen north. However, this girl's speech was not homegrown. In a way, the strange accent gave her more allure.

I answered her, "When I need a break from my studies, I sometimes come here. The cathedral carries so much symbolism to me. It unlocks tension, calling forth the deep instincts of primeval Norwegian life. Why are you here?"

Although I certainly appreciated the fact that she had drawn up a chair near me, I could not understand why she had zeroed in on meeting me. It was flattery. I surely did not want her to end the initial contact. Victoria was a beauty. Over the few brief minutes, I had guessed that she was probably two years older than my sixteen. That only added to the mystery.

"Oh, I work some days at one of the flower stalls outside the cathedral. I have an older relative who does the buying from the wholesaler. Occasionally, she needs time off. If the blooms are ignored, the flowers being perishable, profits disappear. Most of my customers are elderly. When I saw you, because of our ages, I was curious, and I wanted to meet you. Nobody steals flowers, so I left the stall and came in to meet you."

I exclaimed, "I am glad you did."

Victoria asked, "What if, when I close up the flower stall, we go for a walk?"

I had no desire to terminate the meeting. Still, I had to go on duty at the hotel front desk shortly. I explained my situation to her. I spoke very frankly that I wanted to see her tomorrow. I told her where I worked, necessitating that I could see her before I went to work any afternoon. I was so grateful that she immediately nodded her head in understanding.

We agreed to meet the next day at the paved plaza on the harborside of the church. I left her, although I certainly did not want to go. That evening was spent trying to limit my mind to my studies. It was impossible.

The next afternoon Victoria and I strolled along the sidewalks from the flower market all the way down to the waterside. After leaving the snarled connector roads leading out to highway E-6, there was less traffic throwing up dust in our faces. The gentle fresh breeze coming off the fjord felt stimulating to the face. The walk gave us an opportunity to talk without interruption.

I straightforwardly asked, "Where is the origin of your Norwegian accent? I think it lends a certain mystery to your speech that is delightful."

Victoria threw back her head, tossing her blond hair over her ears, and responded with a coquettish grin, "Ah, you see, my father was born and lived in Murmansk until the beginning of the Great War. When the Soviet Army pushed the Germans out of the northern part of Norway, he stayed in Norway. My mother was from Honningsvag. They married there. He worked on the fishing boats and on the docks near the town center. My mother stayed with me at home until I grew a bit. Then, she worked in the small general store one block from the wharf near the beginning of the road out to the hospital. I guess my slight accent comes from my father."

Not dwelling on her speech, I responded, "I know the area of Honningsvag. In all the years of riding the Hurtigruten (the coastal express boat system), when the ship stops there for a short time to off-load freight, I always take that opportunity to stretch my legs. I walk along that only road out of the main, central area. I can never walk very long because the ship never stays more than an hour."

Victoria questioned, "Will you be staying at school all year?"

"No. I think I will be working somewhere along the Nor-Cargo warehouse in Kirkenes for the summer," I answered.

With a twinkle in her eye, Victoria laughed, "If we are still friends by that time, I will get some of my father's relatives who work on the old rusty Russian fishing boats to drop packages off in Kirkenes for you to transfer down to me here in Trondheim. Since my paternal relatives are still in Russia, only lately with the thaw in the Cold War have I been able to enjoy much contact with them. Like all Russians, they are quite poor. For you to send their packages to me would be a big help."

Days had passed. My relationship with Victoria had cemented into a warm and habitual sojourn.

Suddenly one night I abruptly awakened from what I thought was a sound sleep, but obviously was not. My head throbbed. My back, chest, and neck were wet with perspiration. I did not have to search through my memory to isolate my alarm. It was a vivid realization. As clear as a bell, I knew my nightmare was real. The linkage with Victoria had gone on too smooth. Her initial contact with me had been planned. She did not innocently draw up her chair next to me in the cathedral.

This was just the thing that the Oslo agent had asked that I report to him.

I wondered what time my contact would be in his office in Oslo the next morning. I could not conceive of any reason why I should not go on to my early morning classes, and then telephone him before lunch between my classes. However, by morning I could not stand it any longer. Just on the chance that he may be in the office early, I phoned Oslo.

A secretary put my call right through to him.

Before I had time to tell him the entire story, he interrupted me.

"Listen closely. There is an SAS plane out of Trondheim before noon. Pack only what you absolutely need. At the airport gate for the flight to Oslo, give the attendant your name. A ticket with a boarding pass will be given to you. The government is buying your ticket. It is alright to check your bag. I suggest that you limit your talking to anyone. Certainly, make no mention to anybody in Trondheim that you are leaving nor where you are going. Just get out of town quietly and quickly. Do not ask a friend to take you to the airport. Catch a taxi. I will meet you in the airport building in Oslo. Now go . . . and be quick!"

I had not even shaved.

You can imagine my surprise when late in the afternoon my mother and Leki walked into the room with me. We were housed in the government safe house in Oslo, out of sight of the general public. Leki had explained to me that they had received a panic call from a Mr. Storrusten, my agent, just after he had talked with me earlier in the morning in Trondheim. Mr. Storrusten had given them much the same instructions about leaving with haste.

At that time, Mr. Storrusten walked into the spacious parlor.

"I think it is time that we dine in the next room. Over a good dinner, I think I can justify why I have so boldly interrupted your day," Mr. Storrusten explained.

He led us into the dinning room where only a table for five persons was set. The room was enormous. It could have held more than thirty persons. I could see that this site could have been used for banquets of state in years past. As we sat down, two waiters magically appeared. A full five-course meal was ceremonially presented. All of this coincided with Mr. Storrusten's lengthy explanation.

"Ivar, the Government of Norway wishes to personally thank you. You do not know it, but you have come pretty close to being killed. I have yanked your mother and Leki out of Kirkenes for their own protection. You see, we have been shadowing an international drug ring for years. We could never isolate a complete trace on the full routes of their system," he volunteered.

Turning to my mother, Mr. Storrusten continued, "Your son stole a bag of cocaine from a pallet on the dock in Kirkenes. Ivar did not know that it was cocaine, worth a fortune. He scattered it to the wind in the church graveyard. When the pallet that was supposed to be carrying only fish arrived in Bergen, the load of fish was sent by the refrigerated air carrier to the Rome, Italy, airfield. Picked up there by the drug ring, they quickly determined that the drug inventory had been short-changed. Retracing the route of the drug from Murmansk, to Kirkenes, to Bergen, to Rome, the criminals immediately centered on the policeman in Kirkenes. He was probably seized, taken out into the Arctic Ocean, killed, and was dumped overboard. If he had not learned of the presence of drugs, they did not know. Maybe he was part of the ring. But, they could not take a chance."

Turning to Leki, he continued, "Leki, your mother had been a Norwegian agent. Working for the Norwegian authorities, she was considered one of our most prized and inconspicuous agents in the north. She was our eyes and ears. Nobody would have suspected a single mother with a small daughter to be in the intelligence service. When she was killed, we implicated the town policeman, but we could never explain why nor how he had committed murder. We waited. We waited. Finally, we caught suspicion of the drug importation into Europe by a northern route."

His head turned to me and he continued, "Ivar, you triggered panic into the drug ring. They must have felt that they had a defector. They could not eliminate the town constable from potentially squealing. If he were not part of the mafia, then they thought that he had discovered the cocaine, wanted to siphon off some for his private sale, and would resort to blackmail. He had to be killed. In his last moments of life, we do not know what he told the gangsters. Ivar, he may have suspected you. Leki, he may have killed your mother after a bout of lust and rape. She may have ventured into finding out that he was involved in an importation crime ring. Anyway, she never had a chance to tell us."

Mr. Storrusten explained, "Ivar, when you called me this morning, telling me about this sudden appearance of a girl, Victoria, who had introduced herself to you in the Trondheim Cathedral, we got suspicious. If she were a component of the drug ring, then they had traced you down as the only person who had departed Kirkenes in the past three years. If her father were Russian, we do not know. We have not traced that back yet. Whether he was or was not, we do not fit the pieces of the puzzle into the future of a Murmansk connection proposed by this girl, Victoria. Possibly she wanted to get you so involved that you would be compromised. I do not know. If we pick her up right now, we do not have enough to implicate her just yet. Once she realizes that you are not in Trondheim, maybe she will panic. If she is a good plant, she will lie low and do nothing. If she is not a plant, she will do nothing other than reassess her failure at seduction. Ivar, we here at the Bureau feel that if we follow our instincts, you were and still are on the sharp edge of being killed. If the gangsters can get to you, to your mother, or to Leki, then they figure that they have to eliminate you. We can not take that chance."

By this time, my mother was pale. I was soaked with perspiration. Leki was in a state of shock.

My mother, putting her hand to her mouth, said, "But, what will we do?"

Mr. Storrusten continued, "We will have a government barrister clear all of your belongings out of your house in Kirkenes. No explanations will be given to your neighbors. The people at the Rica Hotel will be told that they should not expect you back. Your house will be rented and the Norwegian authorities will place the funds in a bank account in your name. Your worldly goods will be shipped to an assigned holding warehouse in Oslo, known only by our Justice Department. Later, it will be sent to your new address in a safe haven. Likewise, Ivar, your goods in Trondheim will be sent to Oslo. The school will be instructed that you have left. You will lose all scholastic credits, but you will see that you will vastly benefit in the long run."

His assistant chimed in, "You would not be the first to have been murdered by this group. We need to protect you for appearance at a future trial. Believe me, we had to pull you all out quickly. The incident of Victoria means they were hot on your trail. They probably did not know how much information you possessed. However, they could not gamble."

My mother interrupted, "You mean we cannot go home?"

Mr. Storrusten frowned when he said, "Not only that, but we need to get you out of Norway. We do not know the extent of their network. Norway is only four and a half million people. Without a doubt, all of Europe is within their scrutiny. Just changing your names and putting you in a different village is not enough."

Shifting his position in the room, he resumed his plans, "You will all be sent by a government plane to Amsterdam. Under all documents and papers, you will be sent by KLM to New York. Because of the length of the passage, you will overnight in our accommodations near JFK Airport. The next day you will board a United Airlines flight to Chicago.

At O'Hare Airfield in Chicago, all three of you will step on an Air Canada flight to Calgary. I am sorry for all the transfers, but it is done for a purpose. In Calgary a Mr. Thorrsen will meet you. In the Norwegian Consulate in Alberta you will be given a further briefing."

At this point Mr. Storrusten's aide filled in, "Understand you are in the employment of the Norwegian government. Your new life will be subsidized comfortably. Our Justice Department needs you. Furthermore, we have so few people in Kirkenes. Leki, you will be carrying on your mother's tradition. Mrs. Enge, when you return to Kirkenes sometime in the future, all of your friends will learn the truth about your service."

Mr. Storrusten interrupted, "And as for you, Ivar, you will be enrolled at the fully accredited University of Calgary in their highly acclaimed school of petrochemical studies. Norway's present and future economy rests on her partial ownership in the North Sea oil beds. I have no doubt that Norway will be surveying in the coastal areas of the Arctic for future oil and gas. You are essential to us, especially with your deep knowledge of the Finmark coast. I predict that you will repay Norway many times over with your contributions to your country's economy. Ivar, I will go so far as making a statement. At some point in time, I would expect the Norwegian people to recognize what you will have accomplished in your lifetime of service to the government in the drug fight, in your development of petrochemical fields, and in your loyalty to our icebound arctic regions. Representing our frozen areas, I predict you will be elected and will serve in our Stortling (Parliament)."

He paused and took a breath. Then, he gestured with his hand to the north. "Your warmth as a true Norwegian will melt the ice of our northern shores. The ice will change into water. Water will sprout out life . . . a better life for all our people. Norway has in its arctic lands so much ice and so few people. You are one of our precious commodities, our future. From ice to water, from water to life, that is Norway's future. I thank God for you, Ivar."

CHAPTER EIGHT

Glorious indeed is the world of God around us,
but more glorious the world of God within us.
There lies the Land of Songs;
there lies the poet's native land.

—*Hyperion,* Longfellow—

MR. THORRSEN MET US AT THE AIRPORT IN CALGARY. HE IS A tall, straight, flat-bellied man nearing seventy years of age. With his neatly trimmed white moustache matching his full head of white hair, he projects an elegant figure, almost statesmanlike quality. In the past he had singlehandedly done our King of Norway a favor. Our monarch had rewarded Mr. Thorrsen with the position of Norwegian Consul in the western province of Canada, headquartered in Calgary. His duties included many trips back to his home country. Over the years, Mr. Thorrsen became beautifully fluent in English and became a valuable Foreign Service officer as Calgary developed into a center for oil and gas production.

He was to become our guide, our aide, our friend, and my mentor. He had the innate ability to recognize our homesickness, having been down that same road when he first took his post. He understood the inner workings of our individual brains. In a select fashion, he was sensitive to each of our personal troubles. Because of his age, because of his grandfatherlike qualities, he had the ability to sift difficulties down to those that only mattered. At first, to all three of us, Mr. Thorrsen represented our only link to the Old World.

"Realizing your lost feelings in your new surroundings," he exclaimed, "I have taken the liberty to secure the authority of the Consulate Office to permit me to rent you a house. Please understand that it is not necessarily a permanent residence. Once you learn Calgary, you may decide to move. However, it is not proper to put you in a cold hotel room. The house I have selected is furnished. I will help you acquire any other needs that the house requires."

Of course on the drive from the Calgary airfield into town, we were all concentrating our attention on our new scenery. Although we were fatigued from the lengthy trip, the rush of adrenaline kept us alert. We were amazed at the enormous size of the roads, at the cleanliness of the city and of its parks, and at the size of the houses in the residential sections.

As we entered the areas where people actually lived, it dawned on us that now we would be part of this. Separately and individually, we realized Mr. Thorrsen's comments about renting us a house. We felt totally defenseless in our new world. His actions had blessed us, giving us a nest.

Turning in a driveway, Mr. Thorrsen said, "This, for now, is your new home."

My mother gasped. Even from the outside, she could see that our home in Kirkenes was outclassed by the size of this place. With rich soil, the grass and shrubbery bespoke an elegance to the mind that gave my mother an appeal, even before she got out of Mr. Thorrsen's car. As we walked through the front door, all three of us had the rush of an emotion engendered by a mixture of fatigue, of relief, of satisfaction, and of rapture. We could not help it. We all began crying. Mr. Thorrsen cried with us. He, too, remembered the same emotions he had felt when this same moment had come in his life. At that point, he was cemented into our family in our minds.

My mother was like a child in fairyland. As she held out her hands, going from room to room, it was as if symbolically her open arms would absorb her new surroundings into her heart. She was obviously pleased. Momentarily, her home in Kirkenes was blotted out of her thoughts. However, that is the only time when she was completely without Norway in her mind.

"It is so wonderful. It is so big. Mr. Thorrsen, how can we thank you? Why, you even have groceries in the pantry and milk in the refrigerator! How can anyone be so thorough? Ivar, you will not need to sleep in an upstairs attic," exclaimed my mother.

My mother continued, "Mr. Thorrsen, I'll bet your wife helped plan all of this."

Turning his head away, he said, "No. My wife has been dead many years. She suffered long enough from breast cancer. She is in a better house than this."

Changing the subject, he resumed, "Tomorrow a consular aide, a lady, will be out here with an automobile I have leased for you. It is not new, but it is in keeping with our Canadian needs. With all three of you on the consulate office payroll, you will be able to keep up with the payments. The lady will go over all your duties, help you get Canadian driving licenses, help you get required insurance, and assist you in your new life. I imagine that will take several days. She is well versed in this. You will find her most helpful. Right now, I will leave you. Get some rest. And, do not worry. We have all trod this road. You are still Norwegian. You are all employees of the Government of Norway. You have not cut your ties with the homeland. You were sent here for a purpose. In the meantime, we will make the most of our adventure. You will be protected."

We each selected our own bedroom. Sleep did not come easily. Although we were fatigued in our body, our minds were racing.

Leki cried out, "Look, I even have a television in my bedroom! We can polish our English by watching TV."

"Go to sleep, Leki," my mother exclaimed.

In five weeks we had learned much about our new Canadian surroundings. Yet, time had not soothed the scar in our hearts. A longing for the bleak town of Kirkenes elbowed its way into the thoughts of all three of us. It was certainly not the fault of Calgary, nor the blame of the people on the Norwegian Consulate staff. We were kept busy every minute with our duties or with the learning process of adapting to a totally new environment.

If I were to classify our adaptation, I would say that Leki showed the most progress. She made friends easily. Her eagerness caused those about her to react with an unrestricted enthusiasm. She received all the social invitations she could handle. The whirlwind of activity was magnified many times over when one considers that Leki had been raised in northern Norway where life is not exactly a beehive. To Leki, however, I must commend. She seemed to keep everything in the proper balance. To the young men, Leki held the exotic allure of a Scandinavian maiden needing the care of the Canadian good Samaritan. I took great delight in seeing Leki skillfully sidestep the advances of the cowboys from the Canadian Rockies much like the effortless dodges of the master

Spanish matador. The splendor was in watching the majesty of the ballet, knowing full well that Leki had had little practice.

My mother was lost. The house was too big. She did not know the city. She could not understand the immensity of the nation. The churches were too large. Even if she could understand most of the English language, she could not fathom the provincial colloquialisms that were sprinkled throughout everyday speech. She felt guilty when she considered receiving pay from her own beloved Norway for doing no work by her standards.

To my mother, the worst was in not knowing the future. She knew that she could never adapt to Canada to the degree that she would be happy. Without a carrot dangling in front of her face, she dreaded soaking the pillow every night with tears.

Consider her situation. She had been uprooted from her home. She was without a husband. She was sent in haste across the Atlantic. I was virtually raised, even if I was in her presence daily. Those items, worldly goods gathered over a lifetime, that had formed the foundation of the nest were packed in a cold warehouse someplace in Oslo. She wondered if she was ever to see them again. Just to run her fingers over some insignificant item from her house in Kirkenes would have given her comfort. Then, in the next breath, she would have taken to uncontrolled tears, realizing the memories lingering in an aura around the subject.

I am convinced that this is part of being a woman. Possessions, like the mother bird selecting the twigs of her nest, become part of her very being. As much as her own bones, these worldly goods assimilate into her image of herself. To remove these articles from her is an act of virtual amputation.

I could see no cure for my mother's unhappiness.

A man thinks differently. At age sixteen, I consider myself a man. My concern is for the conceptual future. Material items occupy the image of tools that enable me to reach a goal. The sentimental attachment to gears and wheels is lost when my scope is cast beyond the horizon. My vision is to the mental evaluation of the system boding to a life of happiness, blended with a comfortable mixture of service to others. I am not so much concerned with the articles along the way, as I am interested in the complete breakthrough of spiritual growth in the concept of life. Maybe I voice it this way due to my youthful age; maybe I will mellow as time goes along. That is the way I see life currently.

Right now I have so much to learn. Canada is a big country. The environment is so totally different. Every minute of my day is occupied. The pace of life is frantic.

The Norwegian Consulate Office in Calgary, by official communique, was informed that it was now safe for the three of us to go home. That is all that was contained in the notice. We felt like we had barely become settled.

As we were in Calgary as employees of the Norwegian government, our salary being a virtual subsidy, we felt that we had no choice. Of course, we looked on the news as a reason to celebrate.

Leki probably was the one with the most hesitation. Having seen the outside world, she had swiftly acclimated to Alberta. She had looked on the adventure as the advent of good times. Now, to think about going back home to Norway, she had time to run a mental comparison. Especially in the very north of Norway, a young lady would have little to occupy her days. She knew all the young men. She had grown up with them. In Calgary Leki had been exposed to the glamour of the raw frontier, to all the young men, and to the exciting opportunities in the bustling province. Still, she knew that she was tied to my mother and to me. Kirkenes was her home. She could not think about such a drastic act as cutting the umbilical cord from her roots. Mentally, she was fully committed to going back with us. Leki did not even question whether her job at the consulate would be discontinued if she decided to stay.

Although confused and in a state of total shock, my mother heaved a sigh of relief. When we were forcibly transferred to Calgary for our own protection, my mother never adjusted to the move. Certainly, nothing was wrong with the transfer. Kindness and consideration had been shown to us by everybody. Yet, my mother's heart was in Kirkenes. There was absolutely no question in her mind about returning.

She said, "I hope that the government lawyers have not rented nor leased my house. I want everything to be in the exact place that I left it in when I stepped out the door. I want nothing to be changed. I want to go back to the job at the Rica Hotel as if nothing had ever happened. I want to talk with my neighbors as if I had only been on a lengthy vacation."

Condemning herself to a lonely and single life, my mother felt the overwhelming draw of the tundra along the shores of the Varanger Fjord. Kirkenes was her life. She was going home.

The allure of the Canadian West fell into a respectful second best with me. Granted, a life in Calgary presented the thrill of adventure. I could mesmerize myself thinking about the Norwegian settlers of yesteryear, making a new life for themselves on the slopes of the Canadian Rockies. The unlimited land stretching as far as the eye could see was in sharp contrast to the fogbound shore, the granite coast of the Arctic. Whereas in Canada, a young man was not limited with what he could do with his life, in the Arctic he was severely constricted. Not only was the severe cold stifling to all human activity, the opportunity for development in all walks of life historically had never existed. That was the pure hard fact.

Still, one has to have stood in the still of a frigid arctic night to understand the invisible magnetic draw upon the very soul of a man. The feel of nothing out there sharpens the senses. Darkness in the winter strains at the eyesight attempting to form images that are not there. The dense cold air magnifies sound waves as they travel on undisturbed impulses to the undefiled human ear. Kirkenes, being so far above the tree line, has no sounds of the forest to contaminate the air. With man standing in that environment, his ears seem linked directly to the neurons of his inner being. His sense of smell is honed by only one aroma, the sea. Anything else reaching his nose is a signal from the remainder of the alien world. It is as if mankind is surrounded by an invisible field, a protective aura, that once learned, serves as a sixth sense. If one departs the Arctic, this sixth sense is forfeited. Upon returning to the Arctic, animal life regains this instinctive gift.

Only when standing in the polar regions, only when gazing at the heavens from the viewpoint of the top of the world does one get the opportunity to witness the Aurora Borealis. The phenomenon is caused by electrically charged solar particles, high in energy content, entering the earth's atmosphere. Seen only around sixty-seven degrees north latitude, one experiences a gift of nature. Man invariably is moved by this vision, knowing that he is seeing far beyond the horizon of any other existing human. The myriad greenish glow across the sky leaves a man questioning the enormous "way beyond" of human existence. It appears as a foretaste of heaven itself.

I guess throughout human dwelling upon the earth, man has always questioned the effects of man on the earth, and reverse effects of the earth on man. It seems to me that the predominance of effects in this case is that the earth has totally dominated man. Only in recent years has the question been advanced that man through his contamination, through his burning of hydrocarbons, through his disruption of the polar ozone layers has had an effect upon the Arctic.

Some people flourish on social contacts with others. The energy transfer between human beings in a close community resembles the activity in a beehive. Vital to their sense of well-being is the daily invigorating effects of group learning. Much the opposite is true of the arctic Norwegian. Growing up in the upper region of the Finmark province, I am stimulated by aloneness. The silence of solitude sharpens my thought processes. In the far north, to listen and to not hear anything is to hear much. If the hearing is not external auditory waves, one's soul detects a deeper meaning. It is like the illumination of the mirror of the soul. In the Arctic, one knows the immense difference between stillness and silence. True inner growth only occurs during periods of absolute mutism.

As I contemplate my return to my homeland, I instinctively know that Norway is where my happiness lives. Kirkenes is my home . . . I am Norwegian.

CHAPTER NINE

*I never knew so young a body
with so old a head.*

—Shakespeare, *Merchant of Venice 4.1*—

NOTHING HAD CHANGED.

My mother loudly exclaimed, "It is all just the way I left it!"

We had entered our little house in Kirkenes. The community was the exact same village we had left when we had been hastily removed. Our minds were tempered with the ego that a remote township, enduring over hardships of time and of ice, would abruptly suffer alteration when we had left. The three of us were relieved that every stone was in its exact place.

If we had thought the process through, we should have known that the far north acts as a buffer to change. Glaciers move but at undetectable speed. Man's world sometimes thinks that his earth depends on his existence. For Kirkenes to remain as we had left it, we were grateful.

Because of the cold, deterioration is slowed. Oxidation is delayed. Rust is hindered in its relentless march. It is human life that maintains the same timetable. Kirkenes was the same.

I had questioned my original Oslo agent when we came back into Norway through our capital. My mind was puzzled about how fast we had been removed from the country, how little time had passed before we were given the permission to return, and what had altered the situation in the current state.

He told me, "You can only suppose how great was the danger to require us to move as swiftly as we did. You were marked for assassination.

We had been working on the case for over two years. The entire scheme broke overnight. Kirkenes was the link for the importation of drugs into Europe. In the final throes of its existence, the mob killed off more than we were able to round up. You will not be able to learn who the criminal representatives were, either directly or by association. It is not in your best interests to know. You see, we still plan to subsidize the three of you. We need eyes and ears in Kirkenes. You will serve as our intelligence modules. For you to function freely, you must not be clouded by prior assumptions."

That answer did not make any sense. If the mob had killed off the many that the Oslo agent claimed, then why did the federal authorities need to subsidize the three of us? If the drug functionaries had been vastly crippled or had been rendered inactive, then why would we still be useful as intelligence tools? Why would our past knowledge, why would our past assumptions effect our ability to make judgment calls? What made the decision to reinsert us back into Kirkenes, unless there was still a need? And, what exactly was the need? Had the central government made a bet that we would automatically wish to return to our home in Kirkenes?

I did not voice anything about my doubts to Leki. By this stage in my young life, I had formed the opinion that Leki, although older, only stumbled through life as events came her way. That is not to be interpreted as my not loving her. To me, Leki was a sister. However, Leki did not think in analytical terms. In a way, maybe this trait gave Leki a happier life. She was not bothered by all the second guessing that caused me moments of anxiety.

Nevertheless, I did raise my concern to my mother about the entire scenario—our hasty evacuation to Canada, and then our almost immediate return. When I told her about my questions, she heard me through to the end. She seemed to acknowledge that she understood the points that I had made. But, I sensed that she was entirely overwhelmed by the desire to get back home. She did not want to voice anything in the way of doubt that would delay our return.

I felt that I was left with my doubts, isolated in my male world, looking for dangers that maybe were like the mystical windmills of Cervantes. Kirkenes looked good to me, but I must admit, I was paranoid about every shadow. I knew that I would mentally question everybody. Each occurrence would be microscopically dissected, looking for a hidden meaning.

I even went so far as to entertain the thought that maybe the authorities would be counting on one of us to be wary. Could it be that a sixteen-year-old boy, namely me, would be the one the authorities were anticipating to yield an answer?

My mother voiced her insecurity in a moment of weakness. Of course, my plans were to reapply to the university in Trondheim. It seemed only the natural thing to do.

My mother let slip her true feelings when she said, "Must you return to school so soon?"

Immediately after she had said the words, I could see that she was sorry. After all the turmoil, it was only parental instincts that made her want me to be with her. In the next breath she tried to right her comment.

"It is necessary to seize the opportunity. Without university experience, without a degree from school, you will have a dull life here in Kirkenes. You have crossed the broad Atlantic. You have seen Canada. You have visualized the world beyond the frozen expanse. You are a member of the next generation. Of course, you must go."

I replied, "I thought I was a member of the current generation."

Even that did not remove the stinging realization on both of our minds that my stay in Kirkenes was only temporary.

Back in my old familiar room in Trondheim, I had resumed my studies. When I had finished reading my lessons for the evening, I piled an extra blanket on the bed. It was evident that the cold of winter was coming in from the sea. Darkness came earlier. Sounds across the water of the harbor had the crispness brought on by the density of the chill. Life in the town was winding down earlier day by day. Traffic thinned out as the shopkeepers closed doors. Business did not warrant remaining in the stores. All of the cruise ships had stopped making Trondheim a port of call. The flower market outside the Nidaros Cathedral disassembled itself for the winter. Only the basic industries continued to function. Fishing, timber, raw construction material, and farm implements were the remaining active market. Government sponsored activities, education, transportation, communication, and social services kept the people busy. The fields along both sides of the Trondheim Fjord that had been verdant with grain in the summer months were now brown following the harvest. Geometric tracts of land were being overrun by tractors, reconstituting the residual stalks back into the soil to compost the earth.

Although it seemed like northern Norway was preparing to enter into a restful stage of hibernation, my mind was focused upon a winter devoid of distractions, a period of ardent study, and the concentrated mental growth only allocated to the young. I had dedicated myself to making the most of my opportunities, having taken enormous strides in just the short period of time since the interruption by the mandatory sojourn in Canada.

Having finished reading in the textbooks for the evening, I settled under the added blanket on the bed. I do not know how long I had been asleep. All I understood was that my mind and my body were totally at rest.

The telephone rang.

The sound waves penetrating the cold night air caused all creation to protest this abrupt invasion of darkness. My ears heard the ringing of the telephone, my mind registered the auditory signals my brain received, but my cognitive faculty held up its ineffective protest. In the darkness I reached out a groping hand. As the telephone came into range of my ear I heard an unfamiliar voice.

"Ivar, this is the depot manager at the Nor-Cargo warehouse in Trondheim. We have just received a radio communique from the authorities in Kirkenes. Your mother and a girl named Leki have been reported as missing. We have been given no other details. The last part of the message requests that you telephone contact the front desk at the Rica Hotel as it will be manned around the clock. I am sorry, but that is all the information I have."

A chill went through my body even though I was encompassed by the blanket. My mind immediately shifted into sharp focus. I could not imagine what would be the untold part of the message. Having called my mother at the front desk of the Rica Hotel for many, many years, I dialed the number from memory. A woman's voice answered the telephone. I recognized her speech as being a neighbor.

"This is Ivar. What is happening? I am in Trondheim. I received a call from the local Nor-Cargo agent," I responded.

My mother's coworker sadly said, "Ivar, nobody has seen either your mother or Leki for the past day. We have checked your house. We have scoured the town. We have no reports from any shipping vessels. Believe me, the whole village has been searched. We do not know what to think."

I spoke, barely recognizing my own voice, "I will be on the first SAS or Braathens flight leaving this morning."

As I was hanging up the telephone, I knew that I needed to make another call, regardless of the hour.

A sleepy voice in a government office in Oslo answered.

"Please take down this message and see that it gets to the named agent as soon as he is in the office. This is Ivar Enge. I am leaving Trondheim. My mother and the girl, Leki, have been reported as missing from Kirkenes. Is this related to federal agency knowledge or governmental function? Please contact me when I arrive in Kirkenes."

As I hung up the telephone, I have never felt so alone in my life. Obviously, I hoped that this was all an exercise for naught. But, I knew that two women did not disappear unannounced in Kirkenes without terribly bad connotations. I knew that for my mother and for Leki to go without some notification was contrary to reason. Such a rare occurrence might happen in other places. However, in Kirkenes with the approach of arctic cold, no individual, male or female, ventures out without some advance plan announced to somebody. The fact that both women had left without a trace fixes the happening as bad . . . horribly bad.

As I shoved necessary items into a bag, I thought about how I had done the same thing just within the recent past on the family's escape to Canada. I could not help but think that the two events had to be related.

Awaiting the morning at the Trondheim airport, my mind turned to God. In my worry and in my despair, I said a silent prayer.

"Dear God. You know me as Ivar, Takk Gud. I am lonely. You created me and caused me to acknowledge that name from my early childhood. I have thought of myself as being named for 'Thanking God.' I beg you, do not abandon me now. Take my mother and Leki under the safety of your arms. As Jesus is our Saviour, protect them from harm. Please let this cup pass from me."

I hoped that all of this nightmare were a hoax. I wished that by the time I arrived in Kirkenes my mother and Leki had walked casually and unconcerned back into the village square. Yet, I knew that this was highly unlikely. Kirkenes and the area surrounding it were way too small for someone to be missing, to go undetected, to be wandering away into the frozen elements, especially someone from the local town. My mother and Leki were not the venturesome type. They would have no reason to go off exploring. Neither of them had an interest in the fjord, in the old nickel mines abandoned years ago, nor in the inactive Soviet checkpoints. I am certain that my mother had seen all of these areas during her lifetime. Anyway, these regions were not in her field of interest. Leki is a homebody. The only time she would go off into a remote area is when the activity was part of a picnic. Neither had an interest in fishing. I can not conceive of them getting on a boat voluntarily for any reason.

The more I thought of them being missing, the more worried I became.

Without a doubt, I could not separate their situation with all the events of our recent past—the drug packages, our short displacement to Canada, our neat but unbelievable subsidization as intelligence agents. I even thought that maybe the chain of events could retrace all the way back to Leki's mother, and to the old Kirkenes constable.

The airplane trip consisted of a flight that stopped temporarily in Tromso before continuing on to Kirkenes. At this time of year the passenger occupancy was low. Students were back in school. Businessmen were winding down sales trips. All inventories were already warehoused for the winter. The northern areas of Norway were way above passenger traffic related to the oil and gas fields of the North Sea. The fishing industry had little personnel transfer and if they did, they usually went by the coastal marine express system. Still, I remember very little about the flight. My mind was in a blur of worry.

Many times in the past I have walked the trip around the headwaters of the fjord from the airfield to the village square. But, this time I had my suitcase, the weather was cold, and I wanted to communicate with Oslo. Local minivans met all flights and I caught one of these. Actually the one I picked was driven by a long-term friend. He was quick to say that he was sorry to hear of my sad situation. I took this to mean that nobody had heard from my mother nor Leki.

Before going home, I stopped at the Rica Hotel to make my telephone calls and to get the latest reports. In the small lobby were three uniformed Norwegian soldiers. They were all very young, probably in their early twenties. At their side were the standard issue NATO rifles. It was obvious that none of the weapons carried the black cartridge magazines. It was not uncommon that Norwegian troops, always small in number, would be quartered and fed at the Rica. In no way did the presence of the soldiers alarm me. And, I certainly did not link the troops' appearance with the missing women.

Immediately, the woman behind the desk, a coworker with my mother, came around the counter and placed her arms around me. Stifling tears, she expressed her concern. The lady guided me around the corner to a room used as the manager's office.

"Ivar, you can use this office to make your necessary telephone calls. Already there is a message on the desk from a man with the government from Oslo. He seemed urgent that you return his call. When I talked with him, he said it was alright for you to go to your house, but that I should reserve a room for you here in the hotel. We will feed you. I will go out and close the door so that you can make your calls."

I asked her, "So, nobody has heard from my mother or Leki?"

She responded as she turned her face away from me, "No, I am afraid not."

A week had passed since I had arrived back in Kirkenes. I was living at the Rica Hotel, taking my meals in the lunch room off the main lobby. The eating area was quite public. Nothing in Kirkenes is really private. One can hardly move about without being noticed. This fact only made my mother and Leki's disappearance only more remarkable. I felt free to move about as I wished. I had gone to my home many times, both during the day and during the night. However, like my instructions, I never spent the night there. In a way, I really did not want to sleep at home. It would have been too painful.

My time was spent replaying every event I could think of, going all the way back to my early childhood. I retraced my steps. In my mind, I visited every scene. Nothing made sense. I went over and over everything I knew about Kirkenes and the town's strategic global importance. I relived the insignificant games I had played as a child. I wandered over the old stone excavations where the Germans had their guns. The caves had not changed. The same moisture on the rocks had supported the green algae, no different than when I was in elementary school. It was all the same. Nothing had changed.

Although the wind off the fjord was brisk, I had bundled up in heavy clothing. My climbing over the stones, my anxiety, my frustration over the lack of clues, all led to the formation of some perspiration. Resting on the stone steps of the Soviet soldier's statue, I thought back over how many times I had enjoyed childrens' games right at that very spot. My mind wandered.

I tried to ponder the source of dangers. Injury had come to us. Our lives had been disrupted. People had been killed. Even now, I felt that my mother and Leki were probably dead. Too much had transpired. Everything pointed to drugs, to a hideous cartel involved with greed, not caring what evil had to be inflicted on innocent people. I did not know the characters. I did not know who was involved. I could not identify my foe. Without a doubt, my foe knew me. I could not fit the pieces of the puzzle together.

In my helpless state, I gazed up into the eyes of the Russian soldier depicted in the cold stone. The monument was meant to commemorate the proud liberators of the Norwegian north. They had given us freedom. Then, rather than stay in Kirkenes as an occupying army, the Soviets had retreated back to their own soil. Their action had given us liberty.

I fixed my vision on the symbolic eyes of the monument. If drugs had come from the Soviet side, surely that was the source of my danger. But, another thought crossed my mind. The face of the stone statue stood immovable looking towards the southwest. The look penetrated down deep into the territory of Norway.

The subliminal meaning could not be missed. I had never considered that the drug managers could possibly have infiltrated the agencies of the Norwegian government. From a thoroughness standpoint, the placement of "moles" in critical positions either by buying their cooperation or by blackmail was certainly possible.

Now I did not know what to think.

Could my contact in reality be a double agent? Could the sudden eviction of my family from Norway have been part of a dodge, allowing some component of a scheme to be put in place? Why were we suddenly permitted to return to Norway? I could not ever remember anyone being enlisted and subsidized as intelligence gatherers with little or no guidance. If we had been roped into a mesh, why were we in the net? What had we come close to seeing that made our foe so uncomfortable?

My slight perspiration had changed to a brow of sweat. The mere thought of my Oslo agent as being part of the conspiracy terrified me. How was I supposed to conduct myself, not knowing nor trusting anyone? I had to stand up. Like the stone monument, I turned my eyes towards the southwest. My vision went over the drydock where Russian trawlers were getting urgent repairs. Beyond the shipyards, I could see the low hills where the planes took their approach pattern to the runway. Then in the distance, my sight fanned out into the vast nothingness, a composite of frozen arctic granite outcroppings.

It was plain that Kirkenes was an inaccessible fortress, a creation of geography. As an outpost at the base of a tongue, the Varanger Fjord, Kirkenes was snuggled up to the Soviet border. Limited by intolerable weather, all traffic could be closely monitored by the sea, by the one airplane corridor, and by the one road leading south along the Tana River. This fact of geographic handicap would be a perfect site for a criminal element to infiltrate component parts to a distribution system for all of the European continent. Although I had grown up in this very spot, the thought had never been brought home to me quite as clear as when the Soviet stone soldier silently glared in the direction of my enemy.

I shuddered when I realized that my Oslo agent could well be a turncoat whose very soul was owned by the mafia.

If this were true, had the mafia bosses decided to isolate me as a trapped rat in the one place where it would not look suspicious, in my hometown of Kirkenes? Were I to be placed in storage for some unforeseen use later on in time? Had my mother and Leki been killed so that I would be more prone as a brainwashing victim? Surely, they would assume I would be more mentally unstable and likely to comply tacitly with any of their demands.

As I stood at the base of the statue, I wondered if I were having paranoid delusions brought on by my stress. I knew that I had to control my emotions. At age sixteen, I did not know where to turn. It was obvious to me that any misstep, that any deviation from my usual activities, would invite close scrutiny by friend or by foe. I had to regroup my feelings.

CHAPTER TEN

The heart of the wise is in the house of mourning;
but the heart of fools is in the house of mirth.

—Ecclesiastes 7:4 —

UNDER THE STILLNESS OF THE NIGHT, I SAT ON THE FRONT steps of my house. I had to leave the confines of the Rica Hotel. Living in the house I grew up in was so different now that I was alone. Occasionally, wrapped in layers of clothing, I needed to brave the cold. I found that I could think better outdoors, especially when I needed to converse with God. I had to make decisions since no word had been received from my mother nor from Leki. I had determined that I needed to go on with my life. I was in no emotional frame of mind to return to the university in Trondheim. I had taken a job at the Nor-Cargo warehouse at the dock. I wanted to be close in case any news arose in the Kirkenes area.

On this particular night I felt the need to talk with God.

Into the still, cold air I mouthed the question, "Why me, God? I will go anywhere and I will do anything, if you will return my mother and Leki. God, you created me. But, why have you placed this cross on me? What have I done to cause this turmoil? I know that I can not run forever. I want to stay in Kirkenes. I do not even know my enemies. I can not bargain with my God. But, I need guidance. I am Ivar, Takk Gud. I thank You for life. But, hold my hand. Give me a sign. Let me know something. Give me wisdom. You are the Creator of life, but this is bitter. Take my life from me now. It is better to die than to wander about in this aimless mourning. I want to withdraw to the abyss of death."

Out of the vacuum of the arctic air, I heard nothing. I sat on the front steps until the cold jarred my senses out of the depth of despair, bringing both my mind and my body back into awareness. I felt like I had talked with God. However, I was not certain that God heard my prayer. Faith led me to think that God had heard me. Yet, my mind of this world told me nothing. I had heard nothing. God had not answered me. It seemed like my lone conversation had been a monologue, a soliloquy into the thin air.

Trying again, I said, "Lord, I am under the same stars that rendered vision to Moses. I see the same moon as Jonah. You guided the wise men across the sands of the desert. You have permitted me to understand the pain of Job. Lead me through this misery. Come close and support me. As Jesus is my Saviour, change my unbearable state."

The harsh cold penetrated me to the very marrow of my bones. As I sat on those steps, all the world seemed frozen in time and in space. It seemed like it was just God and me. But, I received no feedback from God. I felt His presence. However, I heard nothing.

I had to go inside from the cold.

◈

My daily routine became boring. Minutes became hours; hours became days. No greater diligence had ever been applied to surveillance of all freight being sent either in or out of the Nor-Cargo warehouse. Nothing looked suspicious in any way. No more packages resembled the chalky white powder I had spread over the graveyard. Either that occasion had been a false alarm or it was a one-time-only shipment. I wondered if the shipper of potential drugs had become wary, had stopped using Kirkenes as an avenue port of entry, had eliminated my mother and Leki as a signal to me and to the authorities, or whether some authority in the government had been penetrated by a mole.

My mind was confused, my thoughts were muddled, and my brain could not decipher why I was left in the picture. There had to be some strong reason why I was not wasted. I was operating under the assumption that my mother and Leki had been murdered. My unknown enemy either was counting on me doing nothing, or was anticipating me making some move on the chessboard. I could not understand what moves were available to me nor what my enemy would stand to gain by my actions. Furthermore, my foe had the advantage of seeing the chessboard and I did not.

I pondered. What would someone else predict that a sixteen-year-old boy would do? I reasoned that my foe would do nothing long enough to draw me out of my own backyard. Either I would succumb to curiosity or I would make a mistake and leave the public eye within the confines of Kirkenes. I deducted that I could be attacked and murdered if I left my little makeshift village. My foe had reasoned that any sixteen-year-old boy would sooner or later go to the old abandoned nickel mines, to the now-silent transfer point at Boris Gleb, or into the vast reaches of the Varanger Fjord. Any of those sites was remote enough to kill the victim and to eliminate the body. If Leki and my mother had been lured out together, then their killers or killer had to be capable of destroying both of them. I could not see my mother going into the frigid cold of the fjord for any reason. The illusion of a picnic at the nickel mines or into the forest at Boris Gleb seemed more likely. For me to go to either place, with or without a friend, had to be a fatal mistake. Possibly my enemy counted on me wanting to search both sites. Continuing on with my deduction, my mother would feel less threatened if her attacker were a known and trusted friend. With these unsubstantiated and totally unconfirmed ideas in mind, I felt that I had a weak theory on what might have been. I had to devise some plan once I could identify my foe. There was the distinct possibility that my opponent would only be an agent of my aggressor. Based upon the theory that my foil had committed murder, I was angry enough to assume a "kill or be killed" attitude. Given sufficient time, I settled on a gradual infusion of thallium into my opponent's food or drink. My source was common rat poison. I knew enough about how to handle and to process the dangerous element, if only I had sufficient time and cover to do the job. Another recourse, if I were completely trusting in the local law authority, was to present all my facts to the new constable. Right now, my frame of mind discounted that as a high priority chance. If I were faced with an outright dire physical emergency, in a face-to-face showdown, I doubted that I would have any possibility of winning.

Right now, I had to keep myself in the narrow confines of Kirkenes. I resolved to vary my daily routines as little as I could. I wanted to show resolve, to make my opponent show his hand, and to test the other side's necessity for breaking the current stalemate. I had to be alert for any variation in my environment, in the people of the town, or in comments aimed my way.

Could I kill, if cornered?

Without a doubt, I knew that I could. Even though killing was contrary to all of my inner being, to all of my background as a Christian, I had resolved that this cancer on mankind had to be stopped. Although I so wanted this entire nightmare to end, in the recesses of my mind, I prayed that I did not have to kill.

The other side of me thirsted for vengeance.

Out of the mist from the northern approaches of the fjord came, at full speed, the Russian mother ship, the fish processing plant, surrounded by her four smaller trawlers. All of the vessels were covered with rust. The hulls, the machinery, the navigational equipment were barely serviceable due to basic and to timely routine maintenance. The Soviets neither had the money nor the inclination to do the most meager chores.

What was so unusual was the sight of all the vessels at one time. Occasionally, one Russian ship would come into the Kirkenes drydock facility for emergency repairs when the captain assessed the need to be so great that he could not make the trip all the way around the Kola peninsula into Murmansk, the Soviet repair yard. But, for all five ships to appear at once, and for all of the vessels to be rushing towards Kirkenes at full steam was totally out of the ordinary.

The Norwegian men at the shipyard and around the wharf recognized the strange situation immediately. They dropped their work and gazed seaward. When the first ship tossed a mooring line to the dockhands, a Russian somehow made it plain that all of the vessels had an epidemic aboard. A call was put out immediately by the harbourmaster to the Kirkenes constable. By wireless telephone the policeman gave the order to remove all of the crew, both sick and well, to the town gymnasium for quarantine. All five boats were lashed together and were taken over one hundred meters out into the fjord where anchors were dropped. To the amassed vessels, a fore and aft Bahamian mooring was devised, securing the vessels in place. Knowing that the needs of the exceptionally sick crew far overtaxed Kirkenes' medical ability, the constable radioed Hammerfest for massive aid of both medical people and of biological supplies.

Hammerfest replied that emergency teams would be sent by jet as soon as the crews could be assembled. Prior exercises for just such happenings had been rehearsed over and over on many occasions. Hammerfest suggested to the Kirkenes policeman that the Norwegian authorities be given the priority in notification of the Russian government.

The Kirkenes townspeople were instructed to stay away from the school's gymnasium. The fish stored in the Russian boats was to be ignored. If rotting of the fish were bound to occur, they would simply have to stand any stench. Under no circumstances were the Norwegian people to approach the moored Russian boats. All evidence had to be preserved for Norwegian investigative medical technicians in an unadulterated state. It had to be assumed that laboratory tests may have to be performed on the anchored vessels.

Select people from Kirkenes were chosen on a voluntary basis to pass food and basic services to the seriously sick crewmen in the gymnasium. With diplomatic gentleness, the Moscow government was informed, with full statements about the crew, about the activities that were being assembled to give medical aid, and about the current restrictions for quarantine unless Russian embassy people wished to take an eyewitness look.

Meanwhile, the crew of the vessels suffered. It appears that the epidemic hit those workers on all of the ships suddenly. The first symptoms were headaches. This was followed rapidly with fever, dizziness, and diarrhea. Unable to eat or retain fluids, the crew members became dehydrated. With almost all of the personnel affected in varying degrees, those capable managed to steer the five ships to the closest harbor. The Russian fishermen recognized that this mystery illness was more than the common influenza. They had no swollen lymph nodes. Abdominal pain was generally of a limited type, associated with the frequent diarrhea. Although most of the men were too sick to detect it, those mildly disabled told of a disturbing musty odor to the surroundings. In the breakneck dash for Kirkenes, two men had died. The bodies were released to the sea. Radio messages from the boats back to Murmansk were sent, but it became obvious that the homeport communications people had not sensed the gravity of the situation. Hence, they ran for Kirkenes.

Oslo responded to the news by sending representatives to interview the seamen. Only after the correspondents left the Norwegian capital did the full story develop. The captain of the mother ship rattled off a monologue about the hidden packets of drugs. All the while, his high temperature kept him from understanding nor from remembering what he had said.

The Hammerfest medical laboratory technicians were rapidly securing urine and blood cultures from everybody. Even Norwegian inhabitants of Kirkenes were tested. Throat cultures were added. The lab people then turned their attention to the five moored ships out in the fjord. Cultures were taken of all food, of all water supplies, of any unwashed plates in the galley, and of previously opened cans. The rapidly deteriorating fish were examined and cultures were taken. Having brought a generator and a high pressure washing jet out to the boats with them, the lab men were set to hose down the ships' surfaces. It was at that time that they came across the vinyl packets of powdery white chemicals that the captain had ranted about in his stupor.

The entire haul of what was expected to be drugs was confiscated and was taken to shore. If the substance proved to be contraband, then the ships and the sailors would be considered in a new light. Regardless of the emergency illness, traffic in drugs would be a complicating factor when dealing with the Russian embassy. Safe harbor expectations in marine international law do not give total white paper to brigands.

Although the medical personnel had no proof, although culture results would take time, and although epidemiologists had no tracking of similar diseases, uniformally they were of the opinion that the diagnosis was typhoid. There could be no tags placed on the disease coming from contaminated water from the mother ship or whether the etiology arose from a carrier. Rather than zero in on the little vessels, all signs would point to a source being on the common mother ship where all would have contact. Sanitation was generally poor. Why the epidemic arose after they had been at sea for awhile was unknown. The entire fleet had been at sea with no port calls since leaving Murmansk. Back in Murmansk, and for that matter in the entire north of Russia, there had been no reports of typhoid nor of a similar fulminating fever. The sailors' diet had not varied. They had not employed any toxic sprays. No mercurials were aboard. Of all the people in Kirkenes, none had ever seen a case of typhoid, but everyone seemed to think that typhoid were the most likely cause.

Consequently, and because of the severity of the illness among some of the sick Russians, treatment with typhoid in mind was instituted immediately.

Evidently the treatment worked because fevers broke. Men began to respond to hydration. Headaches and stupors began to subside. One man still died, but the majority appeared to be recovering. The dead man's corpse was airlifted to Oslo without embalming and without autopsy. All in all, the townspeople of Kirkenes felt somewhat relieved. The epidemiologists and the toxicologists remained diligently at work. No release was planned for the Russian boats until final answers were in hand. That included a complete analysis of the confiscated white powder.

As the Russians improved, they were interrogated with a Soviet government agent present. All claimed to be in complete surprise about the haul of drugs. It seemed that no progress was being made until a Norwegian inquisitor reminded the Russian mothership captain that if they were released back into the hands of the Soviet government, things might go much harder for them. Even if their own government over time released them, then they might have some hard answers to give to the questions posed by the Russian mafia. If the Russian captain had suffered no ill will by either his own government nor the mafia, then his sizeable crew might seek some retribution once back on land.

This suggestion by the friendly Norwegian inquisitor struck home with the Russian skipper.

With the Soviet official still present in the room, the Russian captain asked the Norwegian representative, "What kind of a deal is Norway willing to give me for total amnesty, if I can provide details?"

The Norwegian answered, "Norway is not in the business of making deals with drug pushers. We will give you no amnesty. However, as a continuation of pointing out your choices, you can and will be held pending any drug trial. Eventually, you will be released back to Russia. However, the more leads you can give us, the longer it will take us to arrest the criminals and bring them to trial."

By now the Russian official in the room was pale and was in a complete nervous sweat.

The Norwegian inquisitor continued, "Remember the case of Gary Powers who was shot down over Russia in the U-2 intelligence flight. The Russian government had all rights to retain Mr. Powers until he was brought to trial. The Soviet government has set this, rightly so, as an example. Mr. Powers was tried before a Russian tribunal, was found guilty, and was sentenced. He was imprisoned in Russia until finally he was exchanged for a Russian agent held by the U.S. government. In like manner, you will be brought to trial, and if found guilty, be placed in a Norwegian prison. Short of an equitable exchange with the Soviet government, you will remain. However, if a deal can be made that is in the interests of the Norwegian government, an exchange could be bartered. Right now, I doubt if Russia has a Norwegian prisoner that we would want back. Justice probably would be harsh in a Russian jail. To beg for mercy now, to ask for amnesty is a little late. Your best bet is probably the security of a jail cell in a Norwegian prison. Skipper, you are not in a strong bargaining position."

The Russian sea captain's face was lined by his recent illness and by his serious fate. He realized that what the Norwegian had told him was true. Before long he stated, "I want legal representation before I give full cooperation in details as to what I know about the drug running system."

The representative of the USSR had nothing to say. He left the room.

I thanked God. As Ivar, Takk Gud, I was relieved that I was not called upon to seek revenge. I had contemplated killing. Feeling that these people, either directly or indirectly, had murdered my mother and Leki, I was prepared to seek "an eye for an eye." Still, I knew that killing in anger and in vengeance would give me little in the way of satisfaction. I would have lived with the act the rest of my days. It would not have left me. I thanked God that justice was finally coming to those people involved. The cancer of revenge could leave my mind.

Mourning does not walk away as easy. Sorrow lingers forever. I will miss them both. I am alone. But, I still talk to God. Never did I anticipate my prayer to God to be answered in this way. My faith is strengthened. But, . . . my mourning continues, as I live in God's wisdom.

CHAPTER ELEVEN

⚜

I walked a mile with Sorrow
And, ne'er a word said she;
But, oh, the things I learned from her
When Sorrow walked with me.

—*Along the Road*, Robert Browning Hamilton—

THREE YEARS HAD LAPSED SINCE THAT DAY WHEN TYPHOID drove the Russian fishing fleet into the harbor at Kirkenes. Several more fishermen had died before the medicine had stopped the epidemic and before all the laboratory tests had proven the illness to be typhoid. The confiscated drugs had proven to be cocaine. After a lengthy period of legal discovery, the tentacles of the law had gripped many in the distribution system. Those officers in the fleet with knowledge of the drugs had been sentenced in the Norwegian court. Seamen outside the loop had been returned to Russia. Very soon in the search process, the man in charge of the Nor-Cargo warehouse in Kirkenes had been implicated as a transfer agent for the drugs. Before he could be arrested, he had put a pistol upwards in his mouth and had pulled the trigger.

Russia had remained quiet during this episode.

The northernmost province of Norway, Finmark, is so far north of most channels of communication that little had been said in the world press. Even in Oslo, only small notices were allowed to filter into the newspapers. The inhabitants of Kirkenes were rightly upset that two of their own, my mother and Leki, had been killed in the affair. It was never established in the trials exactly who had murdered them, but I think it had to be the warehouseman. No word was ever said about the old constable and Leki's mother.

I did not have any interest in returning to the university in Trondheim. Certainly, the fact that the Nor-Cargo warehouse job fell into my lap did not cement my decision. I was in no mood to try to study anyway. I would like to state that my heart was in Kirkenes, but that was not true. Sorrow had blurred most of my thoughts and my ambition. At age nineteen, to have nobody kills resolve. The house in which I was raised seemed so little when my mother, Leki, and I were squeezed into its small floor space. Now, the house seems so large. Sounds appear to reverberate through the cubic air. Memories are firmly attached to each article. My chain of thought is abruptly interrupted by those remembrances haunting my every waking hour. I am imprisoned by my thoughts.

Food, which should be a joy to a nineteen year old, is merely a ten-minute exercise that I know I have to go through to remain alive. Most of the time I can not recall what I have eaten.

Clothing is essential in the arctic north, but half the time I find that I have walked part of the way to the warehouse before I realize that I am inadequately dressed.

At age nineteen, I understand the normal reaction is to watch the clock. In my case, I really do not care when I go to work, when I leave the wharf, nor when I go home. One thing I am rapidly bringing to the warehouse job is the idea of electronically tying the entire Hurtigruten system, the whole warehouse complex, into a tracking pattern whereby all items stored within the shipping system can be located whether the article is in storage or is aboard one of the freighters. By understanding the current geographic location of each vessel via the satellite positioning system, a proposed arrival time can be projected for each item shipped. This should theoretically lessen the amount of shelf time and of storage space needed in the chain of the transportation line. By having this information ahead of time on an interpolative basis, it would easily indicate when some articles would need to be transported by air despite the additional cost. Although this projection initially costs the system, shippers are happier, products suffering spoilage are less, and insurance rates are scheduled to drop.

Why this has not been instituted in the past, I do not know. I guess it is evident that youth recognizes modern application of advances. Even though I sit in Kirkenes, this plan is being factored into the entire coastline.

Regardless of these things, I am bored, I am melancholy, I am lonely, and I do not look to the future with a sense of joy.

Kirkenes is home. It has its distinct disadvantages, primarily because of its weather and because of its geographical isolation.

However, to someone born in Kirkenes, the town has big pluses. I find that I can concentrate mentally on a problem, not be distracted, and follow the task through to its solution. Having distance from the noise of the crowd makes for clarity.

Still, at age nineteen, I long for female companionship. Because of the small size of Kirkenes, the number of eligible girls is small. I know every one of them. None of them hold a strong fascination in my eyes. When I mentally go over a theoretical checklist, when I subconsciously grade the young women, and when I attempt to place value on them as both a present as well as a future mate, I detect strong stumbling blocks to each and every one of them. Either they have physical attributes that are not appealing to me, or they lack the depth of mental concentration that I enjoy. When I overlay a sense of spiritual emotion to their assets, I find that few remain in the contest. As I go over my wants in a girl, I do not think that I should abandon reasonable desires. Kirkenes enforces proximity beyond most relationships. This ideal girl must possess a brain capable of independent thought. She must be able to seize joy out of meager circumstances. Both to feed on happiness as well as to spread cheer to a mate is essential. Physical beauty is, more than anything, the ability to project warmth and comfort. To enhance this physical beauty is the intangible characteristic of knowing God. As I apply all of these ideal requirements to a girl, I find that none of the girls of Kirkenes qualify.

When I find a girl of suitable intelligence, she is often lacking in physical beauty. When a girl has the physical assets, she does not project a sense of brain power. On the few occasions when both needs seem to be packaged in a girl, she fails miserably in the spiritual department.

I refuse to think that I should satisfy my needs in selecting a life-long companion on the basis of compromise. Nor should I view the women like I am walking down the food counter of a cafeteria. I would not want them to think that way about me. Yet, I know that the mate selection process has gone on for as long as humans have been on the planet. Whether we want to admit it or not, each of us is guilty of some sort of selection process.

The isolation of Kirkenes only makes the mechanism of mate selection more critical. Without the importation of distant genes into the pool of inheritance, Kirkenes could rapidly sink into a cesspool of defective progeny. Without the factor of constant nomadic mixture, the Sami would have become extinct. All of Finmark enjoys the dilution of

Nordic, of Sami, and of Slavic blood. Centuries ago when the marauding parties of the Vikings returned to the Norwegian coastline, they brought with them the addition into the genetic pool the assets of the Norman, the Celts, and the Saxon. Running from the plague brought into Norway the genetics of the Goths and the Huns. Trade brought the Danes, the Flemish, and those of the Hanseatic League. As a consequence, even the arctic north of Norway is not a pure strain of people. I will admit the typical Nordic is the predominant stereotype.

Hence, I will admit that I prefer a girl who is tall, fair-skinned, blue-eyed, and blond. Kirkenes demands thought and values placed upon prior planning. The mental discipline of living in the Arctic reinforces using one's brain in a somewhat painful way when one forgets to plan ahead. One does not forget a trek through the snow bracing against thirty-mile-an-hour winds just because an item is needed. Brain power in a woman is valued more so if she can blend into the balance emotional stability. A hundred days of darkness each year causes mental depression. Alcoholism, divorce, and nervous breakdowns are rampant. Unbridled happiness every day is impossible. However, I am suspicious of every girl that shows the least little trait of moodiness. For the converse, I value the girl who can amuse herself with cottage-type activities.

What I seek is the girl who believes in God, the girl who calls Jesus Christ as her personal Saviour, and the girl who can recognize her role in God's creation. This strength I consider essential. I want a mate who can see more in the Aurora Borealis than a myriad of colors in the sky. I want a girl who can accept the Star of Bethlehem as more than an astrological confluence of galaxies. I want a true companion who can hear a baby's cry, not as a plea of complaint, but as a wonderful mystery of life granted only by God.

When I consider all of my requirements, I wonder if I will ever meet the perfect one. Nevertheless, I continue the search. Surely, there is a female out there with the same thoughts. The north of Norway has been inhabited for thousands of years. All of these people can not be lunatics.

When someone from the more temperate climates looks at the treeless terrain, the barren granite outcroppings, the cold wind spray from the waves off the Arctic Ocean lapping against the stones, the lonesome cry of the sea birds on the wing, and the dim sunlight filtering through the frigid air, they see man imprisoned by the elements. When I look at my surroundings, I see earth at its freshest moments. Without the air pollutants, without the mechanical clutter of combustion engines, and without the waste of human overpopulation, I catch a glimpse of earth as it was handed over to man. The majesty of the world trumpets out its dignity as an opera created by God, a song only discernible to a chosen few who can interpret silence as a blaring message. In this opus, I flourish. My mind works undistracted. I see the poetry, a beautiful and rare sculpture that can not be copied by the hands of man.

Unless a future mate has the ability to feel these things in the very marrow of her bones, she would forever suffer a life of continued discontent. She must be able to sense the blending of the Arctic with the spiritual message of the burning bush crying out to her soul. Rare is the individual who can taste the delights beyond the ice.

Nevertheless, I continue to search.

With this incessant scanning comes sorrow. With my mother and Leki gone, I truly hunger for human contact. The routine flash points of meeting people in the usual movements of the everyday world are but a tease devoid of meaning. Like two birds passing on the wing, like two ships passing in the night, like two deaths occurring simultaneously on two different continents, there is no meaning. Sorrow is thick. My sorrow can not be weighed. My sorrow is not grief. Grief denotes having at one time a possession. My sorrow has no length, no measurable breadth. My Eden has no Eve.

In this vacuum I realize that I will probably find an ideal mate somewhat removed from Kirkenes itself, yet not so far away that she would be threatened by the Arctic. A hundred miles distant from Kirkenes may seem a relatively short distance by the European measurement; however, in Finmark it is forever. Chromosomal mixing as calculated by that distance would put plenty of space to eradicate defectiveness from a genetic standpoint. Possibly, within a hundred mile radius, the environment would not be so different as to make life intolerable to a future mate. Eliminating all of the girls I know in Kirkenes, I now realize that I must spend some time in the search by going to the little Norwegian villages down the coastline. Mathematically, there are almost no inhabitants in the inland territories.

It dawned on me that I could use my job with Nor-Cargo to ride the daily freighters leaving Kirkenes southbound, hitting the small hamlets one by one, spending some energy inspecting the freight system. During these short jaunts, in my spare time I would have to overnight in the little settlements, most devoid of hotels, relying on bed space obtained on the local economy. Food would have to be secured from the immediate people. This would put me in direct contact with these isolated inhabitants. Because of their remoteness, they are happy to talk with a fellow Norwegian. Word would spread among the minute communities. I would not seem to them so much as a threatening outsider. I would catch the next northbound freighter the following day back to Kirkenes. I would file official reports with the company suggesting obvious corrections or improvements in the system, be it warehouse or dock remodeling. I would see the condition of the local forklifts. I would pass on comments relating to employee moral. Because of my extreme distance from both Oslo and from Bergen, I could function somewhat independently, instituting my endeavors before awaiting tacit approval by higher powers. Surely, neither Hurtigruten nor Nor-Cargo would object to inspector-general type reports, whether approved by official sanctions or not. If the reports furnished notes whereby system improvements could be made, the company would value the notices. If the periodic bulletins made no suggestions, but only gave reassurances about the current efficiency of the functioning freight line, then somebody at a desk in Bergen or in Oslo would feel good. My remoteness allowed me to start up this plan, knowing that my job in Kirkenes would not suffer, and that initiative on my part would be interpreted by higher authorities in the best of light.

When I began my sorties, it averaged out to three separate overnight trips every two weeks. My days were filled. I had to squeeze in my Kirkenes work with long days. Some of my reports I had to compose at night. I looked on the short trips as a welcome break in boredom and in my melancholy sorrows. I learned about the economy of the small villages. Occasionally, I found a significant item to bring to the company's attention.

Yet, from the inhabitants of the villages bound by the Arctic Ocean, I could glean no interesting girlfriends. They did not shelter their daughters from me. To the contrary, I could detect that they thought of the marketing potential of this visiting Norwegian young man as a possible suitor for their girl. Still, I seemed to be shooting blanks. In the meantime, my bosses in Bergen and in Oslo were delighted with my new type reports. The submissions received at their desks were passed along to their superiors. All in all, it gave the impression that the system was monitored on a continual basis.

Hence, I had hatched a scheme to find a wife, but I had found no possibilities. I had cloaked my plans under the disguise of work. In so doing, I had created a monster. Now, Hurtigruten and Nor-Cargo expected these business bulletins periodically. All I had accomplished was to establish a new chore that was expected of me on a continuing basis.

During one of these information gathering trips I learned of an incident which firmly illustrated how the geography of the Norwegian arctic influences the few inhabitants. It seems that during one of the long winter nights, devoid of sunlight for months on end, a man and wife had a squabble. What started as a petty quarrel grew in the close confines of the small cabin. The husband took a short walk out the door. The chill in the night air cooled his temper quickly. However, the wife who had been cooped up in the small space continued to seethe. When the husband fell asleep, the angered wife hit him over the skull with the household axe, killing him instantly. Because the ground was frozen, she could not bury the corpse. His body had to lay outside, in a state of arrested decomposition until late spring. When inquiry was made for the man by the villagers, the victim's body was found. The authorities charged her with his murder. At the trial, the local jury found her guilty and suggested to the judge that she be duly sentenced to spend the rest of her days confined to the same village, in the same cabin, having to support herself as best she could, and having her only human contact with those benevolent souls who knew her crime. The judge passed sentence as the villagers suggested.

I learned this story one night sitting in the lounge of one of the Norwegian freighters as I was looking for a wife. As you can imagine, the tale brought home the importance of being very selective in picking a mate.

Of course, it is a drastic illustration of the circumstances in the far north. However, the story underlines how life is different here than anywhere else.

When the story was told, all of the Norwegians laughed. But, each one of them knew that the truth was not funny. Under the surface, each knew that it explained why the Norwegian character is so liberal, a live and let live policy, regardless of country, regardless of color, and regardless of culture. Each person sensed their trait of tolerance, knowing that man is created by God to scratch out a living in his little corner of the world, outside the Garden of Eden.

The story was sobering to me. Picking out a wife was serious business. I wondered if I would ever find a mate. I knew that if I stayed in Finmark a wife would have to be selected as conforming to drastic restrictions. Otherwise, I would have to relocate to a part of the globe with which I was not familiar.

As I remembered back to the very short period of time when I saw Canada, I was struck by the extreme wealth of some of the citizens. Knowing that Canadians are taxed, I marvelled how riches can be accumulated. The contrast was so striking to me because, in the very northern parts of Norway, I had never seen such wealth. Now, after a time has transpired and I have gotten a little older, I recognize the difference. If a person has any wealth, he does not stay in the Arctic. Those Norwegians who have a little money, migrate to the south. They end up in Bergen or in Oslo. If the Norwegian accumulates an abundance of wealth, he spends some of his time in an overseas climate.

A sociological shift has occurred in Norway. Because of the harsh terrain and because of the cold, Norway has always had an outward migration of her people. Rarely do people come to Norway on a permanent basis. With the advent of the iron ships and the steam engine, Norway has become a maritime nation. Her merchant marine acts as the freight hauler to the world. Consequently, Norway's sons have been transplanted to the far corners. When the old man who has worked the farm on the sides of the fjord for many generations is ready to yield the farmstead to his sons, the son answers his father in a respectful way. He softly tells his father that he can make more money working on the offshore oil rig in the North Sea for ninety days, than he can make working the farm all year.

The young people watch television showing overseas films depicting life in European and American cities. Norway does not have the allure. Wealth is used to buy a ticket to go elsewhere.

Of course, I know these are generalities. However, I must respect the truth when I am doing something as serious as seeking a mate.

One early evening while sitting at the bar, a smoking area towards the bow, usually occupied by foreigners taking coffee after their evening meal in the main dining room, I was talking with the barmaid on duty at the time. I was speaking out loud on the subject of trying to find a wife in the frozen north. My conversation was not particularly directed to her, although there was no one else sitting on the stools. She was cleaning glasses. Hence, she was a captive audience. I was not necessarily concerned whether she was listening or not.

After a rather lengthy monologue, the barmaid interrupted me and said, "I have had the same problem. My tale is different. Yet, the subject is the same."

She spoke in perfect Norwegian, the accent fitting either Bergen or Oslo. Looking now straight at me, she said, "My name is Sonya. The shipping company somewhat frowns on the crew speaking in conversational tones with the passengers. However, I know that you are Norwegian. I have seen you riding the ships to and from Kirkenes. I, too, feel the frustration of the quest."

Sonya appeared to be maybe twenty-two or twenty-three years old. The striking thing about Sonya was her size. She must have been an inch or two over six feet. Her weight, I would guess, to be about one hundred and eighty pounds. With these dimensions, she was still very, very shapely . . . just big. She wore her long blond hair in a single thick braid down the middle, extending to the middle of her shoulder blades. Her complexion was the typical Norse fair, with cold blue eyes accentuating classic facial features. When she came out from behind the bar to serve sitting passengers their evening coffee, I made notice that she wore flat shoes with no heels. With her height, she did not need further attention to her elevation. However, I did notice that she had rather trim and graceful ankles for a girl with such big bone structure. Her breasts, ample to say the least, put a slight strain on the buttons down the front of her ship's uniform. Regardless of her size, Sonya did carry a trim waistline. All in all, I would say that Sonya was exceptionally good looking, if one could get past the initial shock of her overall size.

She continued, "I work on the ships for something to do. As you might know, we ride north and back to Bergen. Then, another crew takes the ship for a fortnight. This means I have plenty of time off. Since I have no immediate family, I can be my own boss while in Bergen. My expenses are small. Although the ship wages are pitiful, we have no expenses. In port, I spend little. On the ship, working the bar, I have learned that only the Americans are the big tippers. A little flirting, within reasonable bounds, helps the tips. I get by, but I realize that I will not be happy to do this forever."

By this time I was intrigued with this amazon. However much I wanted to spend more time with her, I knew that I should take it slow. I had another day before reaching Kirkenes at noon. If I did not see her before departing the freighter, I would make it a point to see her when she returned. If I did see her, I would invite her for a quick personal tour of Kirkenes, knowing that the ship was only moored for two hours.

When morning came, I looked high and low over the vessel. Sonya was not to be seen. I knew that no one would be on duty in the bar during morning hours. Still, I thought that maybe she would be assigned to housekeeping duties. I methodically walked all the interior corridors of every deck of the ship, checking all of the maids who were cleaning the cabins. Still no Sonya. I resigned myself to the fact that she must have elected to sleep late. I surmised that she was assigned to the late afternoon until just after midnight shift.

Then I felt the little nudge, the impulse of the vessel coming in contact with the side of the Kirkenes wharf. It was time to leave.

Kirkenes looked good to me. Home always projected a warmth that no other place could claim. Certainly, Kirkenes is remote. Yet, it is full of a special charm that only a hometown boy can recognize. It is plain. It is small. It is bleak. And, it is quiet. All of these characteristics serve to amplify whatever mood one happens to be in at that very moment. The rolling terrain cascading right down to the shore of the fjord telescopes all distances in the town to within the immediate field of vision. To be in Kirkenes, one becomes a part of that quaint stage. Consequently, whatever mood occupies one's mind, Kirkenes seems to adapt.

Sorrow dominated the scene today. I do not know what brought the depression into my mind. Still, all of nature engulfed my gloom.

I did not think of hunger. I felt no cold. I was not concerned with making my way to my little house. My footsteps were made in the snow without a particular goal in mind. How could I be going somewhere, when my thoughts had no direction? Over time I found myself in the small anteroom of the Rica Hotel. Weak in spirit, I collapsed into the solitary chair against the wall. From there my view was across to the front desk, the position where my mother had stood for years. What guided me to that place, I do not know. Nevertheless, I sat. It was as if my inner being was feeding upon something totally unseen. Who knows how long I sat there? In Kirkenes, I could have been as invisible as a ghost. Nobody paid any attention to me anyway.

What trigger was activated? What impulse was registered? What sixth sense was felt when I knew that it was time to go? Without thinking, I pulled my extended leg up under me so that I could shift my weight. Unconsciously, I stood. As I pulled to an erect stance, I felt that my entire body had been doused in a refreshing shower.

Walking the short distance home, I wondered if I were losing my mind. Regardless, I felt better. I had no more answers that when I left the boat. I recall that I marveled over how void my mind felt. It was as if the mental vacuum energized my mood.

CHAPTER TWELVE

If there were dreams to sell,
merry and sad to tell,
and the crier rung his bell,
what would you buy?

—*Dreams Pedlary,* T. L. Beddoes—

WITH A CRISPNESS IN THE AIR, AWAKENING IS NEITHER PAINFUL nor dour. Only in the arctic air does one's mind focus immediately. The mental haze of the night before clouds the mind in the temperate climates. But, in Kirkenes I find that I shift into full-speed thought as soon as I am awake.

There are times when I marvel at the clearness of thought, as if during those hours of sleep, my mind had truly not been asleep, but had resolved many of life's dilemmas, only to serve up a fully prepared plate of solutions. Such was the case on my very first morning home in a long while. Kirkenes had refreshed my spirit. I had a complete feast of answers to many of my questions.

Problem number one was how my future with Nor-Cargo could progress. The prior role of a shipping company was purely to haul freight. I had seen how a little modern technology could be superimposed upon the line to better serve the home office. In the clearness of the morning hours, I saw that the real opportunity resided in making the freight line a conduit of high-technology feeding information southward into Oslo, thereby unifying the 1,150 mile coastline from Kirkenes to Bergen into a distance shortened by the speed of electronic impulses over wireless transmission. The system in place could be adapted with ease into the computer-wise world. Northern Norway in the past had been isolated by distance and by cold. Now, the entire country could be enlarged by making the arctic regions as accessible as the nearest fax machine. The wealth of the north has always resided in the minerals and in the fishing industry. Distance and the ignorance of the unknown had cancelled out these riches. Offshore oil, natural gas, and petroleum products heretofore untapped could be harnessed. Much of the developmental task could be performed in the offices of Oslo. One sector of the economy would feed upon the strides of development of the other factions of the market. As the demand for people, as the demand for supplies, as the demand for services grew, the immense areas would blossom around Finmark, around the North Cape, and even down as far as Tromso. The Lofoten Islands could be linked with the rest of the world. Besides the value of materials, the inherent beauty of these areas would be announced to the world. In the minds of people, the north of Norway had been forbidden territory. With this development, the area north of the Vesteralen chain would be opened as one of man's last frontiers.

Problem number two was the enormous shift in the social demographics presented by the advent of oil-related riches into Norwegian society. Particularly in rural and in fishing components of the people, younger persons could abandon the older tasks, could assume jobs on the offshore oil platforms, in the oil supply industries, and in the clerically related jobs in offices in the city. Farms were allowed to go to waste. The boats and docks in the small fishing villages were permitted to rot away. The people began a mass exodus to the cities of the south, especially to Oslo and to Bergen.

Problem number three was the intense cold of the far north. Fraught with long months of winter darkness, mankind is not capable of electively living in the extreme climates. Even with periodic breaks, subsidized vacations to the south did not make up for the suffering of near-polar existence.

Problem number four was of a tangential nature. At a time when the Soviet fleet was stationed at Murmansk, all of the Russian nuclear submarines had to round the North Cape to venture into the Atlantic Ocean. Murmansk had been the home port of the massive Russian battleship, the *Kirov*. Now that the Cold War had disappeared, the need for a balanced presence in the Finmark area was no more. Emphasis on Arctic Ocean early detection, stress on a NATO force to countermand the Russians, and support for intelligence gathering military units could no longer be justified. With the breakup of the Soviet Union, Norway could shift spending to the cheaper needs of the south. People, jobs, military, and supporting industries were allowed to shift to the more temperate areas.

In the brisk clearness of the arctic air, my mind had consolidated these four problem areas into the recognition that the Norwegian north still remained on the map of the globe. Although times had changed, the northern half of the country still existed. Only a shift of emphasis was required in the future. Adaptation of modern technology to the geographic sector was a bridge to the future.

At my young age, I could see clearly that the future held promise. Environmental issues remained. Fishing, lumbering, mining, trans-portation, and communication factors demanded a representation in the North Cape area. Without a doubt, sailing from Hammerfest to Kirkenes one could experience the quiet beauty of pristine earth. The silence, the barren rocks, the ever-present residual snow, and the pure air attested to the mystical magnetism of the northern provinces. Masses of people who had an ability to see beauty could enjoy scenic vacations in a heretofore unvisited part of the world.

I valued my birthplace as a hidden blessing. I could see clearly that I was placed at this site at a distinctive time in history when opportu-nities would inadvertently arise if one could adapt modern technology to the demands of the present. It was up to me to assume leadership of the parade.

I wanted to share my dream. It was as if I had consolidated my thoughts for my future. Before this, I had been adrift. Now, in the briskness of the cold air, I could see my place in the future. My job, my future, my life's work were outlined in ways that I had not understood. I wanted to talk with Sonya.

There was no way that I could categorize a label for the occupation that was my dream. How could I explain this type of work to Sonya? The work, as I saw it, did not have a name. All I knew was that I could envision the work clearly. My role would be that of a consolidator. Using my background, using my birthplace in Kirkenes, using my firm appre-ciation of the arctic region, my knowledge would be to bridge the huge gap between cultures. Oslo and Bergen demanded a firm basis for decisions as related to this portion of the country. But, what would I call my work? I wanted to sit down and to explain my dream to Sonya.

Nevertheless, I felt uncomfortable when I tried to formulate words in describing what I would be doing. I understood the job. If only I could word it correctly to Sonya.

How did Sonya worm her way into my thoughts?

To place myself in front of the cameras, and to position myself in front of the microphones, I had to spend more and more time in both Oslo and in Bergen. My justification to Nor-Cargo was easy. The more effort I rendered to issues of the north, the more tonnage would be funneled through the freight company. Travel, hotel, and tourism related industries relished the thought of a tidal wave of new interest. How long it would take to produce a measurable effect on money-flow in the northern regions was unknown. However, because of the very small number of industries, any increase in the economy would be immediately recognized. My money source continued to be my job with Nor-Cargo. However, it became evident that my time was being rapidly consumed by a variation of public relations lobbying within the communications industry. Radio and television enabled me to gain the geometrically growing numbers of viewers I needed to get the point across that Finmark remained a vital part of the nation.

Currently, lumbering in Kirkenes was at a standstill. The drydock yard had no ships being repaired. The Russian fishing fleet no longer paid provisioning visits to the city of Kirkenes. The planes of Wideroe and of SAS brought in the mail, but little freight. The buses that met the passengers at the airport had been replaced by taxi cabs.

In the news, fears of trouble with radioactive contamination of the air from disasters encountered on the decommissioning of the Soviet nuclear submarines in Murmansk filled the hearts of the people with terror. Replays of the prior difficulty with strontium ninety at Chernobyl, as it effects the metabolism of calcium, continued to ring in the memory of the inhabitants.

My role in the public relations activity was to not let the issues die. I had to be in constant activity before the cameras and before the news industry. My lobbying had to be persistent.

On my side of the issue was the natural patriotism of the Norwegian people. From the days of the retrograde movement of the Soviet Army back into the Kola peninsula, the Norwegians considered the areas around the Varanger Fjord as being part of the homeland. As a spokesman for the towns of Batsfjord, of Lakeslev, of Mehemn, and of Vadso, I was rapidly becoming a hero. As my face was shown on television, it became common knowledge that I was carrying the cause of the arctic people. Swiftly, I gained recognition over the entire country far beyond my young age.

I had to learn new skills.

On one occasion before the camera, I spoke of my mother's disappearance. This was magnified by the loss of Leki. This broadcast was sent over the airwaves to the entire country. Within a short period of time, the sympathy of the Norwegian people made my face instantly recognizable. The man on the street in Oslo came to view me as a friend. The woman, in the kitchen in Bergen watching her television, saw me as a surviving son. The people my age throughout the kingdom valued me as someone of their age group, one who could voice their own hopes and aspirations.

Nor-Cargo called.

"Leave whatever you are doing in Kirkenes. You now have a blank check to be our representative. You are too valuable a property to sit in a warehouse in Kirkenes. All we ask is that you brief us in Oslo on activities you have planned to the betterment of Nor-Cargo," the voice said over the telephone.

At least I still had my job.

The news media demanded to know more about my mother and about Leki. I found that in telling the Norwegian people about my mother's disappearance, I was teaching the people of the big cities what a woman's life was like in the remote north. Leki represented the young who were in the process of inheriting the nation. The girls had difficulty picturing themselves in these isolated hamlets. The country puzzled over a crime of long ago, a crime unsolved to this day. All kinds of interpretations were theorized about what had happened back in Kirkenes on that black day. In so doing, the Norwegian people were inadvertently learning more about their own country.

Then the epic interview came one day when I was being questioned on television, a broadcast that was being relayed up and down the entire nation. This presentation transfixed my role forever as a recognized person. From that day forward, I was no longer just a young man who was in the employ of Nor-Cargo. I became a voice of the northern provinces.

The announcer asked me, "What is one of your earliest memories?"

As I thought back into the recesses of my mind, I recalled that day standing near the gangway of the Hurtigruten freighter when it arrived about noon. I spilled my story, describing the scene as best I could. I told about myself as the young boy who, in all innocence, looked up into the eyes of the strange man.

"I inquired, 'Are you my Daddy?' The grey-haired American leaned over me and placed his hand gently on my shoulder. With a tear in his eye and with a deep knowledge in his heart, he answered, 'No, but I wish that I were. You seem like a fine boy, someone whom any man would be proud to claim.'"

At this point in the television interview, there was a pause. Behind the scene, a flurry of TV directors were calling for more. In the earpiece of the interviewer, many voices were directing him to carry the discussion further. The media managers were in a frenzy, knowing that they had their hands on an unexpected and an unplanned moment. The projectionists in Oslo could sense that they were filming tomorrow's headlines.

"And, what did you say? What did you remember of that moment? Can you recall any more about that occasion?"

I turned full face to the television camera and I said, "I was dejected, of course."

After that statement had sunk in, I continued. I told that in my despair, I stayed confused. I explained to the television viewing audience that I thought of myself as Ivar, Takk Gud. Only much later did I learn my real name. My mother explained that I was really Ivar Enge. However, the name, Ivar, Takk Gud, was the earliest name I identified myself with. Consequently, Ivar, Takk Gud, had precedence in my mind.

With the television cameraman moving around, getting a different angle of my face, the announcer asked, "Is the meaning what I think it is?"

"Yes." I continued. "Not having the benefit of a father, I realized that who I am is really because I am a child of God. I am Ivar. I am Ivar, thanks be to God. I am Ivar, Takk Gud."

The viewing public understood the symbolism behind this tale. Even in the remote reaches of Kirkenes, a Norwegian boy sensed his very being as dependent on the Creator. The people quickly interpolated the scene with all its meaning. In the snowy hinterland, man understands that he is placed on this globe as a temporary caretaker of the pristine and of the precious. In spite of a situation that is not exactly perfect to the viewer, a young boy without a father, he is thankful for his existence. His very being is wrapped up in the name he has inadvertently adopted for himself. He is intensely thankful to God. Even though his mother and his adopted sister have probably been murdered, he bears his thankfulness.

In the magic of television, the interview was replayed over and over. With each new display, commentators were rehashing the moment. They each went into great detail about how they felt that this young man from Kirkenes had given the Norwegian public a microcosmic view of themselves individually and a summary glimpse of the Norwegian people as a whole. Those affected by my story explained that as they watched the interview, they ran the tape across the inspecting eyes of their own life. The television tape was repeated many times over, much like a familiar commercial.

In the streets of Bergen the next day, everyone was asking, "Did you see the Ivar interview? Could you identify with him? Do you think that someone so young could have honestly rehearsed in his own mind the full meaning as voiced by the network commentators? Did Ivar strike home to you on a personal level?"

I found that I was an instant celebrity.

My original intention was to be a more effective lobbyist for the northern portion of the country. By now, however, I was cast into the role somewhat of a folk hero. The public relations moguls of Oslo were on the telephones. Nor-Cargo realized that they had a hot item. The freight line directors were scratching their heads about how to capitalize on their employee's good fortune.

Morally, I knew that the fateful interview was given while I was in the relationship of an employee. Still, my popularity had now far outgrown my usefulness to Nor-Cargo. Nothing was said about my work. I was allowed to drift away from the freight system without anything being mentioned.

If I were allowed to design a dream, never would I have fantasized a situation whereby I was offered fees for just making appearances at certain events and saying a few words. Most of the time it was difficult to establish a relationship between the set event and my personal story. Still the offers came in daily. In fact, the response was so overwhelming that I had to hire a time-management agency that became a dictator of my activities. I was told by my personal managers that the public is somewhat fickle about such matters. Fame is fleeting. If I wanted to correctly establish myself for a more long-term recognizable fame, then I had to squeeze all I could out of the present. Meanwhile, the money continued to knock at my door.

I felt that I was much like the town crier of old; I had nothing to sell other than words deemed valuable today only. I realized that the sympathy of the Norwegian people would wear thin in a few days and that I would not be able to buy attention. I had no true products to sell. I possessed no skills nor services. I did not have the key to anything related to food, to clothing, nor to shelter. I sensed that I was like the comet coursing across the sky, suffering only a glimpse to the beholder.

As the time went by, my efforts were spent on television commercials. I appeared at the celebration of new business ventures. Gala opportunities increased my bankroll. I questioned whether or not it would ever end.

Still, in the back of my mind, I felt almost guilty. Fame and riches had come my way without my producing anything of value. The stories of my mother, the disappearance of Leki, the flight of my family to Canada, all had brought me wealth in a roundabout way. The public of Norway had paid money to identify with this youngster who had seen the hand of God in events that had transpired in his life.

Sonya had seen the television interview. Over time, she had heard all of the descriptive comments as the announcers dissected every ounce of symbolism that was contained in every voice inflection. She was not impressed with the message. However, she learned more about the messenger. Evidently, Sonya was not concerned about my life story. She cared more about me.

We talked at great lengths on the cruises from Bergen back to Kirkenes. Of course, the quickest method of travel was by jet aircraft. Yet, Sonya was aboard the ship. I made it a point to take the sea route.

I learned her work schedule, and I made it a requirement that I was with her every minute when she was off duty. The rest of her crewmates sensed exactly what was in the wind. They gave her privacy when we were engaged in conversation. In time, we knew that we were to be an established pair.

I could not see enough of her. The world continued to revolve on its axis, but I would have never known it, had it stopped.

Obviously, Sonya felt the same way.

We had both traversed this sea route many times. It was advertised as the most beautiful voyage in the world. It is just that. I had often gazed on the unblemished solitude. In the extreme silence, it was as if the earth was speaking in whispered tones, permitting one to taste prized flavors reserved only for the few who are able to value the moment. Mother Earth was emitting vibrations only to those whose antennae were attuned to her wavelengths. If the environment could be man's church, then, this was surely the cathedral.

As the ship motored through the rock strewn passageways, Sonya and I felt our clasped hands tremble as we felt as one with nature. The earth's beauty was vastly magnified by the arctic scene. Although we had been in the same waters many times, we were given feelings never before appreciated. I knew that it was because we were together.

We talked. And, we talked some more. Little flaws in our character and small blemishes in our acts were interpreted as cute endearments. Unique sayings were picked up in our mutual conversation. We discussed the little things. Playfully, we teased. We cajoled. Without a doubt, we knew we were lovers and we acted like it.

Most of the time our talking was in a light vein. However, occasionally we would talk seriously about things we considered important. We evaluated one another. Most of the time, a mere nod signaled total agreement. Nevertheless, a simple question evoked some expounding, be it assention or discord.

Sonya said, as if talking to the wind, "There is loneliness in a life filled with many activities. Although I have been busy, at the end of the day, I feel that I have done nothing. At least, what I have done has no real meaning."

I asserted, "I understand the feeling. In that one fateful television interview, my whole life turned around. I became recognized. I was recognized not for what I had done, but for what had happened to my mother and to Leki. Fame and wealth sought me out, not because of my doing. The Norwegian people placed me on the pedestal of renown because they needed a hero, someone who had suffered because of the remoteness of the north, someone whom fathers could secure as a son, someone whom mothers could shelter with a nurturing spirit. None of this was my doing. At times I felt guilty because of this. There must be hundreds of others out there in the same situation. Why has God smiled on me?"

We bared our souls to one another.

We knew that we were meant to be paired.

CHAPTER THIRTEEN

The world embarrasses me, and I can not dream
That this watch exists and has no watchmaker.

—Voltaire—

NOW AT AGE TWENTY-SEVEN, I AM AMAZED AT WHAT HAS happened since Sonya and I married.

In our courtship, much of which took place on shipboard, I divulged to Sonya how much I loved her, how much I wanted to marry her, how much I wanted to care for her, and how I could now financially support her. She, in turn, explained that she wanted the simple things in life. She wanted a caring husband, a small house, children, and family unity. She emphasized that she had had enough of shipboard duties.

In frank terms, I explained to Sonya that I had no particular job skills. I had made a considerate amount of money in my public relations work. Being recognized by the entire Norwegian television viewing public, I had become the titular head of the tourism industry in the northernmost provinces. This position bridged over many industries, airlines, shipping companies, freight lines, communications, and to some degree, the extraction component of the mining business. This last phase involved support services for the vast petrochemical industry.

Sonya interrupted by asking, "Will you be home any?"

I explained to her, "Because of its strategic position, I think it would be best if we continued to live in my mother's house in Kirkenes. That way I would be home more."

Immediately, I understood that I had made a mistake. If I were asking a bride to live in a house, I should not have identified the house as "my mother's." I would have to forever alter my speech pattern. If

100

Sonya were to live there, I should always have to label the house as "Sonya's home."

I begged Sonya to please excuse my error, fumbling excuses that by growing up in the house, I had always used that term.

I explained, "By not having a father, I could not call it 'my parent's house.' Other than myself, the only other occupants had been Leki and my mother. My concept is, now, to place my wife on a pedestal as the reigning queen of the only building I have ever known as my home."

Sonya reached her hand over and placed it on my arm.

She said, "Wherever thou goest, I will go."

Time had brought us two children, a girl first, then a boy. Sonya wanted so much to name them for individuals way back in her family's background. I agreed. Hence, our daughter's name was Kirsten. Our son's name, Haakon, resounded with ancient Norwegian meaning.

In the clear, cold air of the arctic north, with the pure, healthy foods from the Norse table, and the security of a warm and loving hearth, both children grew day by day. The bonding of the four of us united our household into a picture-book existence.

I reminded Sonya often, "Our love is only surpassed by our blessings."

My job took me away from time to time. Although the magic of the modern world of electronics and telecommunication permitted me to do much of my work away from a central office, still, I had to occasionally make personal appearances. This made my trips from Kirkenes quite lengthy. Regardless, the advantages of jet transportation whisked me to my destination and back with relatively little discomfort.

In the public relations business, listing my home as Kirkenes gave me a considerable advantage. First, Kirkenes was such a small village that it captured the listener's attention. How could anyone be in the public's eye and live in a spot few had ever heard of before? Next, if a speaker is from such a remote area, how could he have a finger on the pulse of contemporary reality?

In the crucial introductory phase of any meeting, be it advisory, be it contractually, or be it in the form of a speech, I automatically had the attention of the audience. I had a lore of exotic arctic stories to use that mesmerized my counterparts. Through continuous practice I learned to weave my spiderweb that worked to my advantage. My influence, my standing in the public relations business, and my income grew far beyond my initial expectations. I realized that my dreamworld bubble could burst at any time. Knowing that my image could be tarnished by the fickle fate of time, I had to constantly hone and polish its luster.

Part of my value as an agent came because of the rapid expansion of my horizon into the international realm. Norway sits at the upper corner of Europe. As a nation, Norway is not considered controversial. The country is thought of as having a charitable role in the event of human tragedy. Representative members of the Scandinavian countries sit on all of the benevolent boards. The world assumes that the Nordic nations will always respond in a predictive fashion. The wholesome image of united family life spreads beyond the current century.

Norway, also, had the wealth resulting from ownership of one-third of the North Sea oil and gas fields. With an exceptionally small, homogeneous population, and no wars in the recent past, Norway had few expenses other than generated by the weather and unfriendly terrain. Being identified as a Norwegian, this automatically placed me in a position which was considered nonthreatening on corporate boards.

Thus, I had a distinct advantage in my business.

Being of a comparatively young age, time allowed me to generate personal power and individual wealth.

Having in my possession the microphone and being in the focus of the television camera, I began to infiltrate a new theme into my talks. I sincerely wanted to develop depth into my image, something that would last, some thought that my viewers would value in their private time. I needed to weigh items that I sincerely valued in my own life. Going way back to that earliest of my memories, I was Ivar, Takk Gud. I remembered asking that man who descended the gangplank of the freighter at the wharf in Kirkenes, "Are you my father?" It was that primeval recollection that seemed to dominate my existence. If I were to be genuine with my public, if I were to be fully truthful with them, if I were to give them part of my inner being, then I needed to share with them my concepts. I needed to teach them time-tested values that bridged nationalities and age.

Religion was my base. I did not want to isolate myself into any denominational theology. I did not want to paint myself into the corner of any particular preamble as to what was proper religion. I did not desire to fall back on any historical theology. All I wanted to promote was the biblical concept of Jesus Christ as my personal savior. I believed in the existence of the Trinity. I felt that, yes, even today, God created the world and that he created generic "man" in His image. I deemed that I needed to voice my belief in the Resurrection. Using the microphone, I determined that I could teach "salvation by grace" to a world that had rarely heard truth in their secular existence.

I fully understood that once I started down this path I might loose my place in the public relations business. Discussing this danger with Sonya, I knew that I had to make the break. Knowing that my sponsors might pull all support from me, I realized that time was important. Sensing this, I had to organize my thoughts in a quick and in an understandable way, in a form that would bridge over many different cultures, in a method that would stand the test of time. But, foremost, I needed to stay with concepts as presented in the Bible.

I felt that the world as we know it today would give me the abrasiveness needed to retain the public's attention. I would not claim to be a preacher. I would acknowledge that I had no formal education in theological thought. I felt that instead of weakening my image to the viewer, I could turn this into a strength.

My message was simple.

As I spoke, I related that I felt the civilized world had segregated religion into a concept of comfortable convenience. Churches had become unoccupied buildings built by our forefathers. In times of crisis, we turned to religion, all the while having second thoughts as to the application of truth. The world's concept of religion had to conform with what would not interfere with the usual and customary. Man wanted his religion to serve him, rather than religion to be expressed as worship of God.

Man in his modern world looked on religion as a metaphor of the three-legged stool. The first leg was the environment. Man needed to protect the environment as a non-replenishable product. Everything required recycling. Man gave no credence to the earth being in the domain of God. The human brain could not accept the fact that if God in his power could create the earth, then God in his strength could care for his product. In the checks and balances of nature, man placed himself higher than man's capability. Reasonable devotion to the frugality of resources made sense. But, to elevate the environment to a virtual cult status made no sense. Nothing is gained except by using common sense as regard the world's resources.

The second leg of the three-legged stool that had come to be accepted fact in the modern world, even to the point of becoming religiously practiced, was the concept of works. Most contemporary religions favored charity. However, Christianity in the Western world had taken the belief to a degree that made it amalgamated into a firm component of religious practice. Man had taken on the thought that it was his duty to eliminate hunger, to eradicate all disease and pain, to render each individual's life to one of equality. Jesus' words, "The poor you have with you always," had been looked on as ancient words that no longer applied in the light of man's current capability. The viewpoint of Western society was so limited that modern man could not accept the fact that existed beyond the horizon. He did not see the vast numbers over the horizon's rim.

The United States, Norway, Canada, and the United Kingdom had all built into their religion the fraternity of a comfortable country club all working together to right the world of its wrongs. Gathering on Sunday, the "good people" enjoyed the effort that they all disguised as holy work. With labels called fellowship, called communion with fellow believers, called sharing of gifts and talents, they set about to correct the fully obvious mistakes that God had made in creation. Man had cluttered the yearly church calendar with neatly labeled drives, with funds against all things abhorrent, with strong campaigns to eradicate evil, and with sessions to cancel human needs. Knowing that in numbers there is both strength, and knowing that in numbers there is recognition of social correctness, the concept of committees was born. The benevolent capacity of the Christian church was sapped by the idea that man could correct all wrongs. Man had erred in the creation of the second leg of the stool. Modern Christianity had gone wrong in not understanding that this was in God's domain.

With limited items of wealth that are given toward the religious segment of the economy, certain factors within the religious community are in direct competition with one another for the limited wealth.

The third leg of the stool making up modern man's concept of religion was in true worship and in the hard study of religion. Since man is inherently lazy, since man is apathetically unwilling to expend the effort, and since ardent study requires will that goes unrecognized, hours spent in worship are neglected. The Bible is neither taught, nor is it read, be it in the homes or in the churches. Solitary hours spent before the open pages is thought of as being strange. Meditation and private resolve on God are not part of modern man's daily life.

Worship is stratified into a structured hour of the week and no more. Sophisticated man considers this boring, unnecessary, and not relevant to his world. He does not wish to think beyond tomorrow. He recognizes no Supreme Being and no eternity. Man, with his self-centered ego, thinks of himself as the top of the heap in a world of spontaneous creation. Until a crises develops, man does not allow himself to think in terms of God. In that frame of mind, worship on a daily basis is not convenient.

Hence, man made in the image of God considers religion as a three-legged stool. Consequently, man does not do adequately what is needed to pay homage to any of the three legs. Nor does modern man place any of the three legs in the proper place. He does not recognize the supremacy of worship. He does not want to acknowledge that man was made solely for the purpose of worship. Charity and good works by man are only attempts to rectify man's concept of what God's world would be like if it were improved. Environmental issues are man's desires to return the world to a primeval status, infiltrating this concept into a Genesis element of religion.

Slowly, I began to use my position in the public relations industry as my means to infiltrate my talks with my concepts of religion. Having income from my own sources, I could speak my mind. When people sensed what I was doing, rather than turn them off, they became more attentive. When their first reaction was paranoia, later they became stronger converts. Rather than push my own beliefs, I urged them to believe in Jesus Christ, to ally themselves with organized religion wherever they were spiritually fed, and to teach their beloved associates to love God. Just as they ate of the loaves and of the fishes, they needed to tend the Lord's flock only after personal worship.

As the public heard my message, coming from someone who was not of the professional clergy, the interpretation was much stronger. My message and its effectiveness in the public relations industry were registered as more effective. Just as my comments on religion were weighed more readily, my endorsement of commercial products was heavily accepted. One entity reinforced the other.

Sonya and the children sensed my new happiness. Although they did not fully understand how I could incorporate both of the tasks into one, they knew what was happening. The remoteness of the Norwegian arctic allowed me to step back from time to time. In the crisp air, I could think better. From a position at the top of the world, it was as if I had a view from a wider horizon. Coming from the far north, the public who heard my voice considered the source, they made notice of the geographic origin, and they were more amazed. No sponsors complained of the tack I had taken. Long before, I had decided that if they did voice disapproval, I would sacrifice their support rather than change my efforts.

Sonya voiced the most common question. She asked, "Do you think that you are doing any good? Can you quote any numbers as to your effectiveness?"

I answered, "Rarely does the man who plants a seed sit under the shade of the fully grown tree."

I explained to Sonya that I did not recognize that I had a quota. I knew of no method whereby numbers could be attached to my work. Nevertheless, I related to her that I felt an inner compulsion to spread my message. Sensing the reaction of the public, I knew that they were more receptive of the Gospel as it came from an unexpected source, from a person who was not of the ordained clergy.

It was gratifying to me to see the puzzled disbelief as certain people searched and searched for an element of monetary gain. When they could not find any request for financial support, they stood in confusion. They were so much of this world that they could not see into another world, into eternity. They simply could not understand.

I refused to be entrapped into worldly causes. Problems related to widely endorsed world concepts I avoided. Socially acceptable efforts I would not comment on, neither criticizing, nor endorsing. In dodging these topics, I returned to the admonishment of reading the Bible, to the encouragement of worshiping God, and to the push for the individual's freedom of choice to choose Jesus Christ.

Although the microphone and the television camera gave me the compounding of numbers, I had no idea about the harvest. Yet, no sponsors left me. If they had, it would not have changed my mind.

Over time, requests were made for me to move to Oslo. Both formal and informal overtures were set before me to sign other contracts in the public relations industry. All of the written documents were replete with multiple clauses written in legalistic language that I doubt even the lawyers could fully understand. Not knowing, and not understanding, I interpreted all contracts as limiting restraints upon me. Hence, as a consequence, I signed none of them.

CHAPTER FOURTEEN

If a man own land, the land owns him.
—*Wealth*, Emerson—

AS I SAT ON THE STONE AT THE BASE OF THE SOVIET SOLDIER'S statue in Kirkenes, I rolled between my fingers a fragment of the moss that forms one of the chief elements of the reindeer diet. That small piece of elementary plant life told an ominous story. On first inspection, one might miss the interpretation. The lichen was a poor example of the usual spongy, green growth found on the granite outcroppings all over the area. The vegetation normally thrived on the moisture found in the potholes formed by the retreating glaciers of the Ice Age. The bit I held was stunted and yellow. It did not have the cushioned bounce. It did not trap the inherent water content necessary for a healthy plant. I had not selected a specimen at random that would be a bad fragment. What I held in my hands was typical of the moss that was growing over hundreds of square miles across northern Norway, Sweden, Finland, and the entire Kola terrain of Russia all the way to Murmansk.

The immediate effect was on the Sami people, the nomadic Lapplanders whose entire existence was tied to the reindeer. With their herds starving, with the cows aborting, with the young so weak that they could not walk to obtain food, the Lapps were facing eminent death of a culture. The Sami could not understand whether the milk of the reindeer was safe. They pondered over the health effects of eating the deer flesh. For as long as written history, these wanderers of the north had lived a life of independence from human-imposed domination. They had never been subjugated by any kingdom. They

108

had never recognized fealty to any nation. They had waltzed away from serving in any army. It was as if the rigors of the arctic cold had been their protective soldiers. Now it appeared that this little moss would be the end to over five thousand years of life. The Sami had never adapted to what most people called civilization. As the final page in the last chapter of a book called life, the Lapplanders were facing the end.

All because of little green moss turned yellow.

To explain the yellow moss, at the conclusion of the Winter War and the continuation of the conflict during World War II, two areas that had been under Finland in 1939 fell into the domain of Russia. The northern area was around Petsamo. This region is west of the Kola peninsula and is northwest of Murmansk. In an area close, only thirty miles, from the Norwegian village of Kirkenes rests a huge deposit of nickel. Using open pit methods of extraction, the ore was scraped from the earth for decades during the Cold War.

Nickel is a metallic element chiefly employed in forming vital alloys that enhance other structures. It is used in electroplating. Nickel yields steel of greater strength. With combinations of nickel, jet aircraft parts are manufactured of lighter weight with far greater life spans. In the space industry, nickel is amalgamated with titanium and with molybdenum to make exotic metals. This newly acquired area of Russia makes the USSR the world's leading producer of the ore.

The vast open pits necessarily became a well guarded treasure. To work the mines, a new town called "Nikel" (Russian spelling) was populated by workers paid at a rate four times that in the central Soviet cities. As one would expect, Nikel became a rip-roaring mining town where the rough men worked heavy machinery during the day and drank for half the night. One could see the analogy of a lawless town on the frontier of the American West. Sins of the flesh were overlooked by bureaucrats who were concerned only with production quotas dictated by the current "Five Year Plan" announced by Moscow.

Enormous smelters were established whose smokestacks dotted the sky, belching thick clouds of polluted waste both night and day. A by-product of the system sent tons of sulfur dioxide into the air. As the arctic winds dispelled the smoke, all of the soil for miles around took on a chilling blackness, a harbinger of death. The sulfur in the air was sensed as a tolerable stench by the workers, a price paid for the lucrative jobs. One result was that birds' eggshells did not harden properly. The hatchlings burst from the shells prior to viability. Only the sea birds far out to the ocean range were given a healthy reprieve. As water runoff from rains and the melting of snow coursed down the creeks and rivulets, the pollution killed the animals in the food chain. Ponds nesting in potholes became cesspools of chemicals.

In the frigidity of the Arctic, life does not regenerate itself like in the more tropical or temperate climates. Huge ecosystems are vastly more fragile. The scars of death are permanent graveyards, monuments to man's indiscriminate rape of the terrain . . . all for the sake of rubles that were devaluing faster than could be imagined.

The runoff eased down into the estuaries going into the fjords and into the rivers. Fisheries suffered. Spawning was altered by schools of salmon habituated by centuries of instinctive reproduction in the same streams.

And, now came the brittle yellowing of the moss that had been green since the dawn of creation.

From Nikel a narrow-gauge railroad was laid over the granite tundra into Kirkenes. This was by far the shortest outlet to the sea. Norway enjoyed a rebirth of its port. To the east and to the south, a railroad was built into the railhead linking up the mines with the vast system of trains that extended over twelve time zones. In the paranoia of the Soviet mind, Nikel was closely guarded; Nikel emitted no announcements; Nikel suffered no inspections by the West; and Nikel permitted no human migration. The checkpoints at Boris Gleb and at Grense Jakobselv were sealed absolutely except for a few clandestine transfers of prisoners/spys away from the flashbulbs of the press.

Although Kirkenes gained economically, it was as if the sulfur-headed bastard child was kept isolated in the frozen room of the north. The drydock of Kirkenes had work. Consumables were smuggled eastward across the border. The arctic berries used in the making of vodka became currency. No longer did the ancient "pomor" trading in furs dictate activity. It was now nickel.

For an estimated piddling two hundred million dollars the behemoth, Russia, had laid waste to hundreds of square miles of her own territory, to her neighbor's territory, and to a Sami culture that had endured for thousands of years.

Two things brought this tragedy to light. With the collapse of the Iron Curtain, there began some incursion of the Nikel area. Photographers brought back evidence of a surrounding countryside that looked like that of bombed-out devastation. The second irrefutable scenes were the pictures from satellites. Space pictures, showing the area where moss had previously been the dominant vegetation, now projected either yellow moss or no surface growth at all.

To the east of the Kola peninsula were the home ports of the Russian Northern Fleet and the nuclear-missile-bearing atomic-powered submarines. As the USSR was now dismembered, with no money for even basic repairs, the boats were resting at their wharves rusting away, most of them unseaworthy. No reports were issued about the method of discarding the nuclear waste into the Arctic Ocean. Norway was very much aware of the pollution scatter. But, what can one do when sleeping next to a giant? Russia had more people in Murmansk alone than Norway had in its land area north of Tromso. Norway, in the north, was beholden to the liberating Soviets in World War II. But, that is not the way the central government in Oslo felt. And, the southern portion of Norway held the balance of power.

The Russians would not cooperate on fishing. No figures were obtainable about their vast net fishing. Huge fleets circling around a mother ship, essentially a fish factory at sea, depleted the once fruitful Arctic waters.

As I sat at the stone base of the Soviet statue, rolling the yellow piece of brittle moss between my fingers, I realized that I was fingering the ultimate devastation of my home. Cold as Kirkenes was, bleak as the winter's darkness on the fjord, forbidding as a tomb much of the year, I had been born here. I had loved the little wooden house where my mother had the window boxes full of colorful flowers during the summer. I had climbed the steps to sleep in the loft as a young child.

I had kicked a soccer ball in the school playground just behind the Rica Hotel. In the summer, I had rested my head back against the ground, watching the sea birds drift effortlessly on the updrafts coming off the fjord. It was in the grotto where the Nazi soldiers had stored ammunition that I had stolen my first kiss.

The earth was big. Even at my age, I had seen much of it. Yet, as insignificant as Kirkenes was in comparison to the land where human beings dwell in relative comfort, I began to see some answers. I started to understand things that I had never seen before. That first of all memories, asking the man descending the ramp of the freighter, "Are you my father?" I could now begin to put some of the pieces of the puzzle together. My mother and Leki had vanished. I had achieved success in the public relations business. Sonya and I had established our happy home in Kirkenes. Our children were growing up in a healthy environment, or at least it appeared good until the evidence of the Nikel waste.

The Lord had given me a deep abiding faith. Coupled with that, I had inadvertently become the mouthpiece of the Finmark provence to the Oslo government. I sensed that I was obviously the only spokesman who had some weight in the Norwegian central scene in Oslo. Without the weight of a population base, without the force of the oil-influenced south, without the economic clout of the cities, I was the brittle yellow moss, the only remnant of the universal deluge in the days of Noah.

I had to speak out. I had to carry the torch. As Moses was to the Hebrews, I had to lead the cause of the arctic domains. Only someone reared in the far north could understand the problem.

My age-old first memory, that question asked to the man in the dark suit at the Kirkenes dock, "Are you my father?" now seemed to congeal in my mind. I would never know my earthly father. But, I now saw clearly my heavenly Father. I felt that I had been given a glimpse of the creation. I was allowed to see how the sins of man could turn the Garden of Eden into the worthless piece of yellow moss. With a force of faith, I could clearly see my role. All my life I had been groomed for the coming events. I had known tragedy. I had been tempered by the cold. I was given success at an early age. I was buttressed by a supporting, loving wife. I had to become a champion for the neglected few in the north. In the halls of the legislature, one delegate could speak for thousands. I could only vouch for a few. Where the people in Oslo wore the costume of tradition, where the people of Bergen furnished the genes for the vast American prairies, where the sons of the Vikings were the inhabitants of Trondheim, the shoreline of the Arctic was as pristine as on the third day of Genesis.

As I was born in this land, I did not own the land; the land possessed me.

CHAPTER FIFTEEN

There's a land where the mountains are nameless
And the rivers all run God knows where;
There are lives that are erring and aimless.
And deaths that just hang by a hair;
There are hardships that nobody reckons;
There are valleys unpeopled and still;
There's a land . . . oh, it beckons and beckons.
And I want to go back . . . and I will.

—*Spell of the Yukon*, Robert W. Service—

"IVAR, WHY DO YOU NOT ATTEMPT TO GAIN A SEAT IN THE Sortling?"

The manager of the Rica Hotel had asked me that question over and over.

I, again and again, answered him the same way. "Haakon, if I became a member of the Sortling, I would have to live in Oslo. If I lived in Oslo, I would not have to drink your terrible coffee every morning. If I did not drink your awful coffee, I would not get this constant stream of comments from you on the fishing economy, on the drydock, on the amount of freight at the warehouse, on the drunk Russians, and on the value of the krona on the international monetary markets. Nobody else in Kirkenes would listen to you. You would leave Kirkenes. I would be in Oslo. The intellectual capacity of the Varanger Fjord would be equal to that of a cod. And you want me in the Sortling?"

Each morning we teased each other in much the same manner. On a serious note, however, Haakon had a wonderful appreciation of the circumstances Finmark was in primarily because of geography. He knew that Norway was a strange country. All of the weight resided in the south. The wealth from petrochemical products was in the south. The frozen northern territory was a stepchild. Haakon knew full well that if I were in the Sortling, or anybody else for that matter, the representative would be dwarfed in the chamber.

I could only exert my weight by being on the outside. Only by being an independent voice remaining in Kirkenes could I wield any influence. Being of no competitive threat to the members in the Sortling, they would seek out my viewpoints.

Not only did I have more influence, I had more income.

I was a Norwegian using the tactics and the influence peddling of an American lobbyist.

Haakon brought up a subject that I had not thought about in years. We had not spent a full day off in the terrain between Kirkenes and Nikel since we were very young. Even then, we had to observe the rigidity of the Soviet border.

Haakon said, "Ivar, what would you think about picking a good weather day, picking a four-wheel-drive vehicle, and go exploring all the way to Nikel. The border is open. It is easy to obtain the minimal documentation. We could easily cover it in one day. I would like to see the condition and the route of the old railroad. The open pits would still look the same. Although abandoned, the old city would give us an idea what the mining town was like in it's heyday. I wonder if the railroad could have been laid over the path of the ancient pomor trade?"

I jumped at the chance for adventure right in the heart of my own backyard.

"I will tell Sonya. We can load the supplies into the car from the general store right on the square in town. Most of what we need, we should already possess."

I knew that in this part of the world, one did not venture forth without emergency supplies, without informing someone of their plans, and without having a portable telephone communication with a base. The Varanger Fjord and the Kola peninsula, being right on the Arctic, had some of the most changeable weather in the world. I respected these facts. Even though this area was home, both of us had heard of many people who had lost their lives in a "whiteout."

It was common knowledge that along the way, at least three Russian checkpoints still remained. Whether these barriers were still manned, Haakon did not know. He did comment, that if their checkpoints were posted with guards, he knew that the Russians did not consider it their responsibility to come to the aid of unfortunate fools who managed to get themselves into trouble.

On a rare day in Kirkenes, when there were high-flying wisps of cirrus clouds giving evidence of high altitude air currents, but with the surface relatively calm, Haakon and I looked back northward up the vast open expanse of the Varanger Fjord. It was as if we could see forever.

The puffins were darting about in their usual busy search for their favorite crag. The terns were playing on the invisible winds, lazily hovering in the air, seemingly without effort.

Haakon remarked, "We have chosen the right day. How often have you seen a day like this in Kirkenes? I have a strange feeling that we are going to learn a lot."

Before long we were on our way. We soon left the asphalt pavement; the gravel road would periodically sink and lift according to the intense arctic temperatures. At the border crossing we came upon a single Russian soldier sitting on a wooden chair propped against the roadside shed. We surmised that he was brought out to his guardpost and left each morning to his boredom. As the smoke curled up from his cigarette, he lifted his face. Surely, he had heard the noise of our tires on the gravel. He did not take a menacing stance at all as he walked away from his huge AK-47 rifle leaning against the side of the outpost. With a blank face he held out his hand to inspect our papers. He certainly did not have time to read anything on the documents before he handed them back to Haakon. From the shack we could hear the lament of ancient Volga music, evidently from a radio. He did not write any form of record nor make notation of our license plates. He gave us a makeshift wave of the arm, indicating that we could proceed into the new Russia.

The road wound its way up and down over granite outcroppings, down into shallow gullies filled with still damp mud, and past infrequent wooden shacks that had long since been abandoned. Most of the old cabins had boards fallen off the sides and had holes visible in the roofs. Haakon remarked that he thought the old buildings were erected as emergency shelters by hunters during the time of the ore extraction era.

He said, "Although I can not be certain, and nobody has good knowledge of the times when Nikel was the rip-roaring town of a hard living group of miners, I can imagine that this entire area entertained the men as they sought diversion by hunting. I doubt that the sheds were constructed by the Sami. They are nomadic, using hides for tents. Never did they stay in one place very long as they needed to keep pace with the migrating reindeer. I think these were Russian."

The further into the region we went, the more desolate the terrain looked. The moss became much more a dull yellow in color. Where the bare soil remained in the dips near the streams, the dirt was black. Not the blackness of a rich soil, but the earth had the enveloping coat of smut, the evidence of years of belching smoke from nickel smelters. Then, down the road we could see a deserted town. Some of the buildings were of two and three stories, made of brick, having small windows that no longer had glass window panes. Timbers from the floors had either rotted away or had been stripped for fuel. The smaller wooden houses were in shambles. Over the entire huge monumental cemetery to man's desecration, we were mentally deafened by silence.

I stood in amazement, knowing that I had spent my life just thirty miles away. But, those thirty miles were like light years in time. Haakon and I pondered over the fact that during the Iron Curtain years, Russians had been here, supposedly well paid by their standards, but really prisoners to a system. Their lives had been gloom, cold, and vodka. We had heard of the murder rate, of the deaths from cirrhosis of the liver, and of the rampant suicides. However, here we stood right in the middle of the town.

I told Haakon, "Now I can see that the absolute border tightness the Russians maintained was primarily to keep their own people in place. If I were here during those years and had been a Russian worker, my every waking moment would be spent trying to figure a way to get out. Although we have lived merely thirty miles to the northwest, that thirty miles was an insurmountable barrier. I can understand how those three separate, run-down, old checkpoints that we passed coming in here would control everything going in the direction of Kirkenes."

Haakon replied, "But, who would guard the guards? Only the threat of death by those ascending the chain of command would keep order."

I did not even want to get out of the car to eat my lunch, an open-faced sandwich made from brown, smoked cheese. The thermos bottle had kept the coffee warm. As we sat in the silence of the car, covered by the sooty gloom of the graveyard, we were aware of the dense gray clouds that had crept into the city. Everything had taken on nature's much darker hue.

I was the first to speak. Haakon was still immersed in his musings.

"I think we had better get out of here while we can! This weather looks like it could cave in on us at any moment."

We had not been on the return journey more than ten minutes when the zephyr began. Not only was there wind, the snow was being dumped in buckets. I was glad that Haakon was at the steering wheel. Snow is one thing. It is not unusual. But, in the Arctic, it can be something else. Haakon could not see to drive. He dared not open a window to try to see the route. The gravel was quickly erased by the fresh whiteness. Mother Nature had not furnished shoulders of the road; the rough stones had no guiding paint stripes; the unimproved roadbed had vanished. Within what I estimated to be five miles from Kirkenes, the car had dropped down into one of the small ditches that crossed what had been a little creek. Only a trickle of flow remained visible. What had been road was now frozen over. The undersurface was glazed and was slippery. The crisp snow hid the treacherous footing.

Even with four-wheel drive, the car came to a stop. The wheels spun. The motor roared. But, nothing happened.

Haakon looked at me. I looked back at him.

As we walked around the vehicle, we knew that we were doomed. The snow was above the hubcaps already. Digging would be of no avail. And, the snow continued to fall in a true "whiteout." We scampered back into the confines of the car's interior.

"What do you think we should do?" quizzed Haakon.

I replied, "Look, we are Norsklanders. A wee snowstorm should not cause us to panic. First, we plan on safety. Our chief danger is freezing to death, which includes staying in this vehicle. If we attempt to walk back to Kirkenes in this blizzard, we will never make it alive. We have minimal survival gear in the car. On this road there will never be any traffic."

At this point we were both out of the car, assessing our situation.

Downstream, up on the barely visible ridgeline, I saw what I thought was the outline of a cabin. It was difficult to make out exactly because of the falling snow.

I asked, "Haakon, do you see what I think is a shack along that rim?"

"I think it is a small hut," he replied, "and I am all in favor of getting there in a hurry."

As we neared the wooden cottage, I thought that I could smell a whiff of smoke. Then, as we came closer, a man appeared in the doorway of the makeshift edifice. In Russian he greeted us. Extending his hand, he invited us into the one room hut that was warmed by a coal fire in a central stove.

Continuing in Russian, I understood him to say that he heard the noise of our tires spinning on the ice.

Early in the discussion, so that there would be no misunderstanding, I told him that we were Norwegian.

Immediately and what seemed to be effortlessly, he switched to using Norwegian.

"My name is Victor. What are two Norwegians doing out in a snowstorm, miles from nowhere? I had no idea that this deserted road to Nikel is now on some tourist route. I welcome you to my home away from home. As you can see, I belong to the wealthy class, those Russians who can afford a second home."

He made the last statement with a gleam in his eye.

Victor continued, "You see, Russians with any sense have dachas on the Black Sea. Many years ago I worked on the fishing boats out of Murmansk. Then, when the ore was being extracted at Nikel, I could make more money in the open mines. I switched from being a fisherman to being a miner. On the few occasions when I could get time off work, a group of us built this cabin as a shelter when hunting. All the other men either died or moved away. Consequently, it is mine. Now, with little work in Nikel, I spend more and more time here. It is very lonesome. I welcome you as my guests. I have warmth, I have reindeer stew, and I have that most Russian of all drinks."

With that comment, Victor held up what remained of a bottle of vodka.

Haakon and I welcomed his hospitality. I knew that nothing was going to harm our car. With the storm, I realized that Sonya would assume that we had sought shelter for the night. Consequently, Haakon and I settled down to enjoy the Russian's offer of an overnight shelter. Even then, I wondered if it would be for only one night.

I explained to Victor that we had made a sightseeing trip to Nikel. Although we were from Kirkenes, we had never seen the Nikel area, commenting that the border had been closed for many, many years.

"Yes, I know," said Victor, as he took another swig from the bottle. "Excuse me." Victor reached down, found another full bottle of the clear liquid and opened the top. "I have a huge supply. It is wonderful to have friends who can enjoy the storm with me and who can drink with me by the fire. It has been years since I have had guests."

Victor hung his head, shaking his face one way and then another. His features took on a forlorn melancholy. It was obvious to me that Victor had started on the vodka earlier in the day. In the dim light, I could see that Victor put his bearded chin on his two supporting hands. I could not be certain, but I thought I could detect a profound mood change in our Russian host.

Outside, although it was still snowing, there were no sounds. Birds and animals had sought shelter. This time of year the sun should have been high in the sky. With the blizzard, however, all of nature had taken on the lifeless gray intensified by ground white with snow. No sun . . . no sun. It would take days for all of the snow to melt, even after the storm had gone past.

Shaking his head, Victor lifted his face. Now I could plainly see that the Russian was truly sad. Living in close proximity to the Russians, we knew of the Russian ability to endure dark moods. Suffering is the deepest element in the Russian character. In their songs, in their dress, in the classical books of the treasured Russian authors, no group of people on the face of the earth can exhibit depression as merely being the normal and expected state of existence like the Slav. It is as if the Russian rather enjoys wallowing in misery.

Victor portrayed this mood in full. With that, he took another swallow from the bottle. He offered Haakon the vodka, but my companion refused.

Shifting his weight on the wooden chair, Victor pulled himself a little further from the fire. It was evident that the vodka was getting him warm.

"This cabin has seen so much sadness," Victor explained. "It is a wonder that I ever come here anymore."

He shook his head, wiped away some tears, took another short swig, and said, "Enough about me, enough about this lonesome hut. Tell me about you." With that remark he looked directly at me.

Haakon merely nodded his head when he looked at me, indicating that he was somewhat relieved that the comment was directed my way.

"Oh Victor, we are just two Norwegians who wanted to see Nikel. I have lived all of my life in and out of Kirkenes. We have families back in town. We thought that when we left early today that the weather would be good. Then this came in rapidly. We are grateful to you that you permit us shelter."

Victor shifted his chair. He remarked again, "This humble cabin has seen so much trouble."

It was clear that the vodka was taking its toll on Victor's mood and on his thinking. He was not listening to me. His mind had not left the forlorn; his wretchedness was in complete charge.

He continued, "All of my hunting companions are either dead or have moved away. In my youth, on the fishing boats, we would stop in Kirkenes for supplies. On days away from the nickel pits, we would come here. This abode has seen many drunk but happy Russians. Now it is no more. Son, do you believe in God? If so, call on him for me. I am miserable. I am only half drunk. Call on God to make me either sober or pass out in my sorrow."

Thinking that my host, Victor, was really asking for my help with his mood, I blurted out that I never knew my father. I firmly believed in God. I explained that for years and years I had thought of myself as "Ivar, Takk Gud." I knew that I existed through the grace of God. I was a child of God. No matter what happened, God was in my close vicinity. He was my father, there to hold out a supporting hand when I needed it.

Victor interrupted, "But, I have suffered so much. Years ago, I had a girlfriend in Kirkenes. We could see each other only on those occasions when my fishing boat came into Kirkenes. I could not stay. Then the curtain closed. No people were allowed to pass across the border. The closure was absolute. For many years, I was not permitted out. It was work, work, day and night in the mines. Years passed. I never married. My love was in Kirkenes. We had not seen each other in years. Then the political thaw came. We could travel."

The bearded Russian paused to take another draw from the bottle. Then, with tears in his eyes, he continued his remorseful lament.

"We would meet in this cabin. She would walk from the border so as not to bring attention to herself. In this shelter we found our long lost love. She told me all about her life. We planned to rejoin our lives. Then, on her second trip to this cabin, it all happened. In a snowstorm much like this, I walked in the door. I walked in the door and found their frozen bodies. I walked in and found my love and the adopted daughter she called Leki."

ABOUT THE AUTHOR

VERNON J. HENDRIX, M.D., IS A RETIRED OBSTETRICIAN AND gynecologist who also serves as a deacon and Sunday school teacher at Second Ponce de Leon Baptist Church in Atlanta, Georgia. He earned his bachelor's degree in biology from Emory University in 1953; he also earned an M.D. from Emory in 1957. Hendrix served as captain of the Korean Military Advisory Group in 1958. From 1960–63 he was a resident at Baptist Hospital in Atlanta; then he engaged in private practice as a physician until 1992, when a stroke abruptly ended his medical career. Since then he has traveled the world on various Christian missions, collecting material for his compositions and ministering to the people he meets through his books. Dr. Hendrix and his wife live in Atlanta. They have two grown children and two grandchildren.